## "There's sti[ll] us, Mary Jan[e]"

Against all reaso[n] into her throat. She pushed it away ruthlessly. "The past is dead and buried, Garrett."

"That's what you think." He stepped forward suddenly and took her chin in his hand. For an instant Mary Jane feared he was going to kiss her again, but he didn't. Instead, he looked into her eyes and said, "I can't figure out exactly what you're afraid of."

Panic blossomed in her eyes. "I...I'm not afraid of anything," she bluffed.

He answered with a derisive snort. "Yes, you are." He leaned forward and grazed a light kiss over her forehead. "And I promise you, I'm going to find out what it is."

**Dear Reader**

RESOLUTION: MARRIAGE is the last book in my *Marriage Ties* series about a family of strong women, the Kellehers. Rebecca, Brittnie and Shannon have all had their stories told and now it's time for their mother, Mary Jane.

Mary Jane acknowledges that she's the matriarch of her small clan, though she's far too young for that word to be applied to her. She is leading a happy, busy life when she is confronted with a man from her past—her old high-school sweetheart, Garrett Blackhawk—wanting to know why she broke off their relationship so many years before. Mary Jane is torn between reawakening attraction to him and her feelings of guilt over a secret she's been keeping from him for far too long... I hope you are as eager to read Mary Jane's story as I was to tell it.

Happy reading!

*Patricia Knoll*

**Recent titles by the same author:**

BACHELOR COWBOY

# RESOLUTION: MARRIAGE

BY
PATRICIA KNOLL

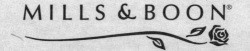

MILLS & BOON®

*First published in Great Britain 1999
Harlequin Mills & Boon Limited,
Eton House, 18-24 Paradise Road, Richmond, Surrey TW9 1SR*

© Patricia Knoll 1999

ISBN 0 263 81887 X

*Set in Times Roman 10½ on 12 pt.
02-9912-49239 C1*

*Printed and bound in Spain
by Litografia Rosés, S.A., Barcelona*

# CHAPTER ONE

MARY JANE KELLEHER STOOD with her hand on the phone. Her fingers curled against the hard plastic until the tips turned white beneath her short, unpolished nails. She wished she didn't have to make this call. In fact, she would happily give up half of her Running K Ranch if she didn't have to. Even though her daughters, Becca, Shannon and Brittnie had been the ones encouraging her to call, she didn't think they would appreciate it if she tossed away half their legacy on a whim.

Sick dread twisted through her and her heart pattered in her throat. She had no choice. Someone had to phone, and by process of elimination—not to mention cowardice on the part of her neighbors—she was the one elected.

For the dozenth time, she checked the number written on the crumpled piece of paper in her hand, although by now she had it memorized. With a deep breath, she picked up the receiver and punched out the digits. When the telephone was answered on the second ring, her heart kicked into racing speed and she had to sit down on the tall kitchen stool so her knees wouldn't buckle.

"Good morning. Thank you for calling Blackhawk Enterprises," said a young, crisp voice. "This is Kay speaking. May I help you?" The young woman's efficiency forced Mary Jane to stop dithering and get on with the reason for her call.

"May…may I please speak to Garrett Blackhawk?" her voice started out as a whisper, then grew stronger. She could do this, she told herself firmly. She could do this if she stayed calm and focused.

"I'm sorry, Mr. Blackhawk is in a meeting. Could I take a message?"

Mary Jane resisted the urge to grab this easy way out. She could leave a message telling him what he needed to know. He wouldn't have to call her back at all. It wouldn't be necessary for her to talk to him—coward that she was.

"It's really very important," Mary Jane said. How much did Garrett's employees know about his family situation? she wondered. "It's, um, personal and confidential," she said, then winced at the trite phrase. She gave her name and number and said, "Please have him call me as soon as possible, and…"

"Oh, wait a minute, ma'am," the girl interrupted hastily. "The meeting just broke up. I'll see if Mr. Blackhawk can speak with you now. Please stay on the line."

The receptionist cut off and Mary Jane was listening to music from a radio station in Albuquerque, where Garrett lived. He owned a huge ranch outside of town and had other business interests in New Mexico's largest city. He was a successful man, the pride of his hometown here in Tarrant, Colorado, but he had rarely been back in the twenty-eight years since they had graduated from high school in the same class and he'd gone off to the army, then to Vietnam, then college, and finally to establish his own business.

She was happy for Garrett, glad that he'd done what his father had said he'd never be able to do—become a success without Gus's help, influence, or money.

She had been to Albuquerque many times over the years, but had never seen him. Had never wanted to see him. Even now she didn't want to. In truth, she probably wouldn't have to. All she had to do was deliver a message, and that would be the end of...

"Mary Jane?" a deep voice rumbled over the line. He paused and then repeated in a tone thready with disbelief, "Mary Jane Sills?"

She jerked and nearly dropped the receiver. Gripping it, tightly, she answered in a breathless tone. "It...it's Kelleher now, Garrett."

"Yes," he said hastily. "Of course, I knew that. I'm just so surprised by your call."

"I know, Garrett, and I'm sorry if I startled you." As if searching for safety, a familiar anchor, her gaze traveled around her kitchen. *Garrett. Garrett Blackhawk, after all these years.*

She could barely focus because her thoughts were tumbling around like the loose marbles her grandson, Jimmy had dropped on the kitchen floor last week.

"You didn't startle me. It's just that I'm surprised." A self-deprecating laugh crackled on the line. "I already said that, didn't I?"

"Yes, I..." She forced herself to be calm and said, "Garrett, I'm calling about your father."

There was a sharp intake of breath. "Why, what has he done? Has he hurt you, or your family? Because if he has..."

"No, no, nothing like that." Mary Jane twisted the cord around her fingers. "He's very ill, has been for months now, but he wouldn't let Mrs. Chandliss call you." The truth was, old Augustus Blackhawk had threatened Ruth Chandliss's life if she tried to call Garrett, but Mary Jane wasn't going to tell him that—not yet anyway. "I think he's had at least one stroke, but he won't go to the doctor to find out."

"When did this start?" Garrett rapped out.

Taken aback, Mary Jane had to stop and think. "Last June, I believe," she said slowly. "That was when we first noticed the change in him...."

"And no one could be bothered to call and tell me about it?"

"Now wait a minute, Garrett. All of us..."

"All of who?"

This wasn't going *at all* as she'd expected it to. "All of the neighbors," she continued grimly. "We felt that if it was a serious problem, one of his employees would call and tell you about it, or that you would come home at some point and check on him," she added for good measure.

"Home?" he asked softly. "Tarrant hasn't been my home for nearly twenty-eight years."

Frustrated, Mary Jane rubbed her knuckles across her forehead. "You know what I mean. Listen, Garrett, I don't know the nature of your relationship with your father, and frankly, I don't care. I'm only doing the neighborly thing and calling to tell you he's sick and he needs you." If it's not too late, she added silently.

"A few months after the fact," Garrett groused, causing Mary Jane to grit her teeth.

"Just as a visit from *you* seems to be a few

months late,'' she added pointedly. Good heavens. In her wildest dreams she wouldn't have expected her first conversation with him after all this time to be one of such acrimony. The conversation was serving at least one purpose: her irritation with him had blasted away her nervousness. "I just learned today how worried Ruth Chandliss is about him. He threatened to fire her, or worse if she called you.''

Garrett snorted. "I don't know why she didn't quit years ago.'' Mary Jane agreed with that, but didn't comment.

"What makes you think it's a stroke?'' Garrett continued.

"His color and appearance are bad. His speech is slurred, his behavior has been very erratic, and…''

"You mean he's been meaner and more irascible than usual,'' Garrett broke in. His tone was harsh, underscored by a note of disgruntled acceptance.

"Yes, I'm afraid so. No one can do anything with him.''

"It's my responsibility. I'll come right away,'' Garrett responded immediately. "I'll fly up.''

Mary Jane's annoyance with him cooled and she almost smiled. Once the decision was made, he moved fast.

He had always loved speed; fast cars, fast horses, a plane instead of slower ground transportation. She'd heard that he'd been a door gunner on a helicopter in Vietnam. She'd found it impossible to imagine the boy she knew bracing himself in a doorway, his basketball player's hands wrapped around a machine gun. Her mind skittered away from that horrifying image. She had to stop this. Swinging wildly from one emotion to another was only making her more agitated.

"Can someone meet me at the airstrip outside Tarrant?" he went on.

"Yes," she answered. "I can find…" She almost said "someone," but there was no reason for her not to pick him up. It was the neighborly thing to do. The *adult* thing to do. "I'll be there. Just tell me what time." It was probably reckless, even stupid to volunteer to meet him, but there were things he needed to know about his father before he saw the old man again. And if he felt compelled to blame her or the other neighbors for not contacting him sooner, she was perfectly willing to give him a piece of her mind. It wouldn't hurt Garrett to learn that the sweet, biddable girl she'd been had grown into a mature woman who ran her own business.

Garrett was going to be shocked when faced with Gus. Even though she thought he'd been neglectful of his difficult father, she could try to soften the blow at least a little.

"That would be fine, Mary Jane. I appreciate it." He told her what time to meet him. Before he hung up, he paused. His bad humor and gruffness faded. His voice was low and sincere as he said, "I know the old man's been rough on you and on your family, MarJay, so I'm grateful that you were willing to call me."

This swift change in attitude had her heart thumping so hard she could barely hear. She answered in a choked whisper. "I felt like I owed you that much, Garrett. For…for old times' sake."

"Oh, MarJay," he said, his voice low and

clipped. "You don't owe me a thing." Then he said a quick good-bye and hung up.

Mary Jane eased the receiver back on the cradle then walked across the kitchen and slumped into a chair. Her breath rattled in her throat as she sat with her hands dangling loosely in her lap. *MarJay.* No one had ever called her that except him—when they'd been seventeen and so desperately in love. It brought a sweet ache of remembrance and a hint of sorrow because they weren't those same people anymore. They were forty-six years old with a lifetime of experiences between them. When they saw each other today, they would find great changes.

She looked at her hands. These weren't the soft, tender hands of a young girl anymore. They were toughened by ranch work, even scarred in a couple of places due to tangles with barbed wire. Standing, she walked over to the small mirror that hung by the back door.

Her gray eyes were clear and steady. Her features had been softened by time and the ten pounds she'd put on over the years as a result of motherhood, muscle-building ranch work, and learning to be a good cook. Her short blond hair didn't show any gray. She made sure of that with bottles of haircolor that her daughters teased her about. She didn't care. She had always taken good care of her hair and her skin. There were few lines around her eyes, so she saw no reason to let gray hair advertise her age.

Her grown-up daughters did that for her.

Mary Jane glanced down at the plaid shirt and jeans she'd put on that morning and decided she'd better change. It wasn't vanity, she assured herself.

These were dirty because she'd had to ride out and pull a heifer from a mud puddle.

In fact, she had time to shower, do a proper job on her hair and makeup, and press the lavender pantsuit Becca had bought her for her birthday last month. Not vanity, she assured herself again. It was common courtesy to look nice when meeting someone at the airport, especially if she'd had words with that someone and wasn't willing to show weakness before them. Besides, she was simply following the rules of good grooming she had taught her children. Satisfied with that logic, she headed for the bathroom.

Garrett Blackhawk sat with his hands resting on the stack of work he needed to accomplish or delegate before leaving for Tarrant. He didn't even give it a thought.

*Mary Jane Sills.* He savored the name, then corrected himself. *Mary Jane Kelleher.* He knew she was a widow, had been for four years. In fact, he knew a great deal about her because he had a subscription to the *Tarrant Times.* He knew about the milestones of her life; the births of her children, the times she and Hal had bought and sold property. Hal's death.

In fact, almost the only thing the *Times* hadn't told him about Mary Jane was why she'd married Hal in the first place.

*Hell.* Why had he spoken to her as he had? Blaming her for not letting him know about Gus's illness? It wasn't her fault, or the fault of anyone else in the neighborhood around the Blackhawk ranch. It was Garrett's fault because he couldn't hold onto his temper long enough to have a five-minute conversation with his father. Garrett called every month and spoke to Ruth, asked how things were, but Gus had probably intimidated his housekeeper into keeping quiet about the true state of his health. He should have gone to see for himself. He knew what his father was like.

Ignoring the work on his desk, Garrett stood and moved restlessly to the credenza against the wall to pour himself a cup of the fresh coffee that his secretary, Jill, kept made for him. Carrying the mug she'd bought him that said ''Boss Man'' in big red letters, he walked to the window. The mug was a joke between them because she told him he was the toughest boss she'd ever had, but only managed to be the fairest one she'd had because she kept him in line. She was right. He didn't argue with the tiny, grandmotherly dynamo who ran his office. Besides, he'd taken the mug's message as a compliment. He didn't mind being tough as long as he didn't turn into a bastard like Gus.

Garrett looked out at the plaza courtyard of the Blackhawk building and felt quietly satisfied with what he saw. The fountain in the center splashed in the September sun, sending sprays of water into the air and reflecting tiny, fleeting rainbows. Employees strolled or scurried across the courtyard, depending on the urgency of their errands, and whether or not they'd noticed him watching from his office window.

The various sections of the three-story building housed different branches of his company. Ranching and farming interests were in one, land development in another, venture capital in a third. The fourth side of the adobe-style structure faced the boulevard, giving a view of the bustling city where he'd lived for more than twenty years. He was proud of what he'd done here. He admitted he'd started out simply to prove Gus wrong when he'd said Garrett couldn't make it without his father's money and influence.

He had made it. He was a wealthy, successful businessman; but he'd never married. He had no family. When Gus died, there would be no one.

Garrett took a sip of coffee, then frowned down at the cup, unable to decide if the coffee was bad or if it was only flavored with his own regrets.

Mary Jane wasn't wealthy, but she had a family, every personal relationship he didn't possess.

He had felt like he'd been kicked in the gut when Kay had told him who was on the phone. He'd picked it up with visions of the young Mary Jane in his mind, only to be taken aback by the mature woman's voice that had spoken to him. Logic told him she'd changed. After all, he had too. He was middle-aged, though Jill said she couldn't detect a hint of middle-age spread. She would have put him on a diet and exercise program if she had. His hair was still black, though silvered at the temples. If he'd had the inclination, he could probably still button his old army uniform, even if his body had matured from that of the eighteen-year-old who'd first worn it.

Garrett released a gusty sigh and turned away from the window. Why in the world was his mind centered on Mary Jane and whether or not he could get into his old army uniform when she'd called to give him the bad news about his father?

A stroke, she'd said. Maybe more than one, and

the old man hadn't been to the doctor. Well, that would change as soon as Garrett got to Tarrant. He turned grimly to the task at hand. But first, he had to clear his desk.

The small jet glinted silver in the afternoon sun as, wings dipped, it circled to make the approach to the Tarrant County Airport.

Mary Jane watched it make its graceful approach, noticing that on the tail the shape of a hawk was outlined in black. When the plane banked for a turn, she saw the words "Blackhawk Enterprises" lettered on the fuselage and Garrett himself behind the controls. Garrett had a corporate jet, she thought with a mild sense of shock. Precisely how rich *was* he, anyway?

She brushed her hands over the front of her pantsuit jacket, then glanced down at her hands, wishing she'd put yet another dose of lotion on them to smooth some of the rough places. Oh, what was the point? It was obvious that she worked hard and her hands showed it. Garrett wasn't here to see her, anyway. He was coming to look after his father. Still, she was glad her hair had turned out well, soft and curling around her face, emphasizing her eyes to which she had applied makeup more carefully than usual.

She shook her head ruefully and leaned up against the side of her white pickup truck, trying to relax while avoiding any dirty spots for fear of soiling the suit. Of course, she could have put on her coat, but the bulky parka wouldn't be a welcome addition to her outfit.

*Vanity, thy name is Mary Jane,* she thought.

With an even glide, the small jet landed on the runway that the Tarrant County supervisors had paid to have scraped out of the weeds and sagebrush on Jasper Mesa, and it taxied to a stop by the small shack in which Red Adkins, the airfield manager, kept track of the comings and goings of the sparse local air traffic.

In a few moments, a door on the fuselage of the plane opened, a set of stairs descended, and then Garrett was standing there. He seemed to fill the doorway, his black hair brushing the inside of the doorframe. A small flight bag and a briefcase were clutched in one hand. He surveyed the area at the edge of the tarmac, spotted her and lifted his free hand in a brief wave before he started down the stairs.

She stared at him, dazed. She didn't remember him being so big. Had he continued growing even after graduating from high school and leaving Tarrant for good? Her gaze traveled over him, taking in the details. He had definitely filled out; his shoulders were broader, his body more substantial and muscular. As he descended the steps, she saw that his tread was solid, not the light dashing steps of the young man who had been the center guard on the high-school basketball team.

Of course not. How silly of her. This was a man, not a boy. For some reason, tears filled Mary Jane's eyes. It took her several seconds to realize that they were caused by regret and sorrow. The two of them had meant so much to each other at one time, and now they were meeting as strangers.

She was relieved when Garrett hurried toward Red's office. It gave her a few moments to take deep breaths and compose herself. She hadn't expected to feel such a punch of emotion when she saw him. She'd better learn to control her reactions quickly, or she would regret far more than the years that had passed.

Within five minutes, Garrett had finished in Red's office and stepped outside, striding briskly across the tarmac to her. Mary Jane raised her hand in greeting, and then he was standing in front of her. Before she could even lower her hand, he took it in his and held it as he looked into her eyes.

"Hello, Mary Jane," he said, his voice a deep rumble that sent a host of memories tumbling through her mind. His hand was warm, strong, wide enough to swallow hers whole. His face had changed, too. It had settled into lines of maturity, his strong chin a counterpoint to his high cheekbones and deepset eyes. When he smiled, tantalizing creases appeared at each side of his mouth. His eyes were still blue, the deep, dark navy blue she'd never seen anywhere else.

She swallowed the lump that had formed in her throat. "Hello, Garrett. It's good to see you again." Inwardly, she flinched at the commonplace greeting, but he didn't seem to notice.

"It's good to see you again, too, Mary Jane. It's been a long time." He seemed to be examining her as closely as she had looked him over, but Mary Jane wasn't as comfortable with it as he had been. She glanced away.

"Is that the only bag you've got?" she asked. He nodded, heaved it and his briefcase into the bed of her pickup, and then said, "I figure Gus will probably toss me out on my ear, anyway, so I'd better travel light." He strode quickly to her side of the truck and surprised her by opening the door for her to climb behind the steering wheel.

Mary Jane, accustomed to doing things alone, stumbled back a step before catching herself with a small, self-conscious laugh. "Sorry," she murmured and scrambled inside the cab of the truck. She felt uncomfortably foolish when his hand touched her arm as if to steady her. He was only being a gentleman. She needed to accept this with a little more grace and stop being so awkward.

Once she was settled, she glanced up and saw Garrett's lips twitch in a tiny smile as if he knew what was going on inside her head. *How could he?* she wondered. *She* didn't even know.

As Garrett climbed in beside her, she started the engine and finally relaxed. They pulled out of the parking area and Mary Jane began to descend the mesa. Garrett looked around. "Every time I come back here, I'm struck by how little it's changed."

"There's not much growth in population here," she agreed. "Because there aren't many jobs."

He nodded and she fell silent again. The tension in the truck seemed to be sucking out the air. Mary Jane flipped on the vent fan. She hadn't expected the strain between them to be so bad, but then she didn't know quite what she *had* expected. This was nothing like the high-school reunions she'd been to where former classmates would rush into each other's arms for a hug. She couldn't imagine doing that with Garrett. She would have felt horribly awkward, and she doubted that he would have welcomed it.

"Mary Jane," he said suddenly. "I was sorry to hear about Hal. He was a good man."

She gave him a sideways glance. "Yes, he was."

"And a good husband, I assume," he said. Oddly, it didn't seem to be a question. He seemed to her to want her to confirm what he was already thinking. That was fine with her because it was true.

"Yes," she said. "The best. And a great father, too."

Garrett was turned half-way toward her, his shoulder resting against the door. Mary Jane could feel him observing her. "I guess that's why you married him so quickly," he said suddenly. "Because you knew he'd make a good husband and father."

Mary Jane jerked and the truck veered toward the center line. She straightened it out and shot a glance at Garrett's face. He raised an eyebrow at her as if to ask what was wrong with her. She returned her attention to the road and gripped the steering wheel with sweaty palms. "Yes," she said. "I did know that. Listen, Garrett, why don't we discuss my family some other time? Right now you need to know what's been happening with your father. Ruth might feel uncomfortable telling you. She's a very loyal employee."

Garrett's gaze held hers for a second as if he was unwilling to drop the subject of her family and reluctant to discuss his own, but he finally gave a self-deprecating snort. "You're right. I've been thinking about my dad the whole way, but now I'm avoiding it. Tell me what's been going on."

Relieved, Mary Jane nodded and launched into a description of Gus Blackhawk's erratic behavior which had begun last June. "He's run a number of people off his place, even threatened a few of them with a shotgun. I think he may have suffered a stroke, but as far as anyone knows, he hasn't been to a doctor.''

Garrett nodded and his face grew solemn. ''He wouldn't, of course. Thinks he knows better than they do.''

''That's what Ruth said.'' Mary Jane slowed the truck. ''Here we are,'' she said unnecessarily as she turned into the driveway of the Blackhawk ranch. She had passed the entrance thousands of times since she had lived on the Running K, right next door, but she'd never ventured down this road. It had been well known that she wasn't welcome there.

Beside her, she felt Garrett go rigid with surprise. He sat up and his gaze darted around the ranch, noting that some of the fences were down, the cattle trailing across the drive. Mary Jane had to stop and toot her horn at them to get them to move, slowly and languorously, out of the way. Weeds choked the graveled drive as if it was rarely used. There were other signs of neglect and disrepair that Garrett seemed to take in with one sweeping glance. She could almost feel the shock going through him. Gus had been nothing if not a perfectionist.

''Ruth says things are pretty bad at the house, too,'' Mary Jane said, feeling that he should be warned about the worst of it. ''Gus won't let her fix anything or call anyone to fix anything.''

They crested the hill and looked down on the small valley that held the house, barn and outbuildings. Even from here, they could see that the place was dismally run down.

"I should have come sooner," Garrett said quietly. "But he didn't want me."

Flooded with compassion, Mary Jane stopped the truck, reached over, and placed her hand on top of his. "I'm sorry it has to be like this."

He didn't answer, but he nodded and after a moment, Mary Jane removed her hand and continued the drive.

When they pulled up in front of the house, the door opened and Gus Blackhawk himself came out onto the porch. She had seen him recently, so Mary Jane was prepared for what she saw. Beside her, she heard an audible intake of breath as Garrett absorbed the sight.

Gus's clothes were torn and dirty, his hair long and unkempt, a gray straggly beard jutted from his chin. He squinted at Mary Jane's truck, then his head lifted to see her behind the wheel. As soon as he saw who it was, his face went stiff with fury. Shakily, he made his way to the steps and started down them, holding onto the hand rail as he shouted, "What are you doing here? You know you're not welcome. Trying to get your hands on what's mine, that's what you're trying to do. Well, it's not going to happen...."

Garrett exploded out of the truck and hit the ground running. He whipped around the front of the vehicle and caught up to his father in a few quick strides. "Dad," he called sharply. "Stop it."

Intent on Mary Jane, the old man ignored his son until Garrett rushed to him and took his arm. Gus started to pull away, but then his watery blue eyes flashed up to meet Garrett's.

"Dad," Garrett said again. "Stop it. Mary Jane brought me here to see you."

Gus's lip curled. "Garrett. It's about time you came home." He lifted his chin. "But you didn't have to bring her with you."

Garrett looked as if he wanted to argue, but he held it in check. Mary Jane saw his jaw clench. "Never mind that. I've come to see how you are."

"A lot you care," Gus said, jerking his arm from Garrett's grasp. He gave Mary Jane one more malevolent glare. "And you get off my property or I'll call the law on you."

It wouldn't be the first time. Embarrassment rushed through her and she wanted to snap back, but she wisely kept her mouth shut. Gus turned and began climbing the stairs into the house. The ill will she felt toward him melted when she saw the distress on Garrett's face. "What the hell's that all about?" he demanded. "I know he hates all his neighbors, but why is he so full of hatred for you?"

"He's always been like that," she said evasively. "Especially when he suspected you and I were dating in high school."

Garrett shoved a hand through his hair. "That's ancient history. Why should he, or anyone, care about that now?"

An unexplainable stab of pain shot through her. She managed a small shrug. "He's holding a grudge," she said.

"It's ridiculous," Garrett said, grabbing his flight bag and briefcase from the truck bed. "Whatever was between us ended years ago. It certainly doesn't matter now." He gave her a distracted glance. "Thanks for the ride, Mary Jane. I appreciate your calling me. I'll see you soon.'' He turned and loped up the steps after his father.

Mary Jane took a deep breath, put the truck in gear, and pulled away. Gratefully, she headed toward home. He was right, of course. What had been between them didn't matter now. In fact, he'd made it clear that things were over between them when he'd left twenty-eight years ago.

Approximately seven months before she'd given birth to his daughter.

# CHAPTER TWO

GARRETT STOMPED OUT onto the porch and took a few quick turns, his shoes thundering on the boards. He wished he was eighteen again and could childishly indulge himself by kicking the hell out of one of the porch posts. He stopped beside the last one where frustration and rage had him gripping it until his knuckles turned white.

Damn, the old man was stubborn.

Garrett whirled around and stalked to the other end of the porch. He'd just spent two hours arguing with his father, trying to get him to go to the doctor. Every one of his arguments had been met with a refusal until Garrett had shouted in fury and stormed outside. He needed to calm down before trying again, but the sight before him only fed his distress.

Standing with his hands on his hips, Garrett stared out at the ranch that had once been the best run in Tarrant County. It looked like pictures he'd seen of it when his grandfather had first bought it during the Great Depression. The whole place had a hopeless, forlorn appearance.

*Much as Gus did.* Garrett grimaced. It was evident to Garrett that Gus was gravely ill. He was convinced that his father had suffered at least one stroke, as Mary Jane had suggested, and probably more.

Mary Jane. He was still irritated that she'd waited so long to let him know about Gus's condition, but

24

he understood it after seeing his father's viciousness toward her. No one had called Garrett because they didn't want to be attacked. Gus had never gotten along well with his neighbors. He'd hated Hal Kelleher because Hal had refused to sell out to him years ago, but even that didn't warrant the attack the old man had launched against Mary Jane.

Garrett admitted that it had shaken him up to see her. He hadn't expected her to look like an eighteen-year-old, and he hadn't been able to imagine her at forty-six. She seemed to be caught in time somewhere between the two ages; blond, graceful, yet with a touch of clumsiness he'd always found charming. She'd been nervous, too, about seeing him.

As well she should, he thought grimly, because there was unfinished business between them.

Garrett's eyes narrowed as he stared, unseeing, at the ruin of his father's once-prosperous ranch. Before he left Tarrant again, he was going to talk to her, he decided. As soon as his father was better and he could concentrate on dealing with Mary Jane, he was going to find out answers to questions he'd had for so long, whether she wanted to answer him or not.

"Garrett!"

He whipped around at the frantic alarm in Ruth's voice. The housekeeper dashed onto the porch, letting the door slam behind her. She rocked to a stop when she saw him and her hands flew out. "It's your father," she said. "He's collapsed in the living room."

Garrett stared at her for a full three seconds before he whipped around and dashed past her into the house. "Call the paramedics," he shouted as he hurried into the living room. Gus was half on, half off the sofa, his arm trailing onto the floor. His left hand and arm were twitching uncontrollably.

Scooping him up, Garrett settled him more comfortably onto the sofa. The old man's head lolled, the corner of his mouth and his eye were pulled down. His eyes rolled in his head, but then seemed to focus on Garrett. Recognition sparked and Gus's lips began to move. Garrett leaned closer to hear what he was trying to say.

"Did…the right…right…thing running her off… Mary Jane Sills…white trash…."

Stunned, Garrett stared at his father. At a time like this, the only thing he could think about was Mary Jane and the argument they'd had so long ago that she wasn't good enough for the son of Gus Blackhawk? Along with his horror, Garrett felt a wave of sorrow and pity at what was still uppermost in Gus's mind.

"You know…I was…right," Gus mumbled. "Was…right." His eyes closed and his breathing grew shallow. Anguished, Garrett took his hand, wondering at the man who had fathered him, a man so entrenched in his beliefs that what could well be his last words were ones of self-justification.

Garrett paced the small waiting room, then sat down on the sofa. He stood again, whirled around, and glared at the thing. It wasn't made for a man over six feet. In fact, he couldn't think of anyone its short back and hard seat could have been made for. Rather than risk a back injury, he would continue his pacing while he waited for Frank Kress to come tell him what was wrong with his father.

He'd been in the way in the examining room, and Frank's scowl had made it clear he wasn't wanted there, so he'd decided to make himself scarce. He needed to think, to try to puzzle out the meaning behind what his father had said to him, that he'd been right to run Mary Jane off. Garrett ran a weary hand over his face.

She hadn't run off. She'd married Hal Kelleher and moved in right next door to Gus. How that must have galled the old man. Garrett knew his father had tried to buy their land, to discredit them in the eyes of their neighbors. In fact, Garrett wouldn't have been surprised to learn his father had resorted to cattle rustling and fence cutting, but he couldn't understand the depth of his father's animosity toward Hal and Mary Jane. Garrett wished he could scrub his father's bitterness from his mind, but it was fixed there, and he continually returned to it.

Looking for a distraction, he glanced around the room. The furnishings were ugly cast-offs from who-knew-where, as if this place where families waited for word of their loved ones didn't matter. Its grimness seemed to be a solemn proclamation to a patient's family. It said, "Expect the worst."

The sick, heavy feeling in his gut told him he already knew what the worst was going to be for his father. Frank would come in soon to say Gus was dying and there was nothing Garrett could do to stop it. Not that Gus would have wanted his son's help. He was eighty-five and determined to die on his own terms, just as he had lived. Alone. Garrett's mother had died when he was five, and, as he'd grown up, he'd wondered if she'd slipped away because she simply couldn't meet Gus's expectations.

Garrett forced his mind away from that thought. No point in dredging up the past. There was enough for him to deal with right here and now. Besides, he'd come to terms with the riddle of Gus Blackhawk years ago when he'd realized he never wanted to be like him. He'd watched the way Gus had treated people—neighbors, employees, acquaintances—and done exactly the opposite. If he'd married and had children, he would have done the same thing.

Garrett knew his father's collapse probably would have happened whether he'd come home and had an argument with Gus or not. Still, he felt guilty for the words they'd exchanged. The added stress hadn't helped. He didn't want to think that he was even partially responsible for this, though he knew he was.

He needed to get out of this miserable room, he decided, turning toward the door. He was getting morbid.

On the way to the cafeteria, he turned a corner by the pediatrics wing and rocked to a stop. Mary Jane was coming out of a room and quietly closing the door behind her. She glanced up when she saw him and froze.

Along with surprise, he saw a flash of something else flit over her expression and darken her eyes to deep gray. Could it be guilt? What did she have to feel guilty about? Intrigued, he searched her face, noting the way color washed over the softness of her cheeks. Then he looked into her eyes and watched her gaze shift away from his.

"Oh, hello, Garrett," she said. "What are you…?" Her face grew stricken and her hand came up to grip his forearm. "Is it your father?"

He nodded, quickly detailing what had happened at the ranch after she'd left. He glanced down at her small, competent hand resting against his sun-tanned skin. He couldn't remember the last time a woman had reached out to him with comfort. How many years had it been since she'd touched him? A lifetime. Distress and apprehension dragged at him and he felt warmed by her gesture of compassion.

Mary Jane listened to Garrett describe the argument with his father, saw the frustration in his face and knew he was blaming himself for Gus's collapse. She wished she could help, but the problems between the two men had probably been blooming since Garrett's birth and might never be resolved.

"What about you?" he asked, nodding toward the door she'd closed. "Are you doing volunteer work or something?"

"I wish," she said, pulling her thoughts back to her own family responsibilities. "No. My grandson is in here."

Startled, he drew back. "Your *grandson?*"

She chuckled softly. "Don't sound so surprised. I've got two grandchildren. Step-grandchildren, really. Becca's children. Her son Jimmy fell out of a tree and broke his arm this afternoon. I'm here with him while Becca and her husband, Clay, go get something to eat. He's asleep now, so I was going to walk up and down the corridor and stretch my legs."

Garrett's dark eyes searched her face. "It seems incredible that you would have grandchildren." He lifted his hand and pointed to her, then to himself. "That we're old enough for that." He shrugged and one corner of his mouth lifted in an ironic look. "Of course, I had no children, so no grandchildren, either."

She flinched inwardly at the loneliness echoing in his voice. Guilt sat on her heart and she looked down, unable to meet his eyes. Hearing movement in the corridor she glanced up to see Clay and Becca approaching. They were studying the tall, solemn man beside her. Becca and her sisters had long been curious about Garrett, wanting to know if he was like his father—it seemed that they were about to find out. Mary Jane's stomach clenched with her worry that they would see the resemblance Garrett bore to Shannon.

"Mom?" Becca said, hurrying up. "Is Jimmy giving you trouble? He's not the easiest patient...."

Mary Jane shook her head. "He's fine. Asleep right now. I'm not used to sitting so much, so I came out here to walk around a bit."

Her worries eased, Becca nodded and returned her attention to Garrett. Mary Jane watched carefully, but saw no sign of recognition from either Becca or Clay. Relieved, she performed the introductions. When they expressed their sympathy for Gus, she noticed a mocking glint in Garrett's eyes. After the way Gus had verbally attacked her that afternoon, he was probably thinking that if Gus treated the rest of her family like that, the authenticity of their concern was suspect. He thanked them, however, and said he was still waiting to hear Dr. Kress's diagnosis.

"I was on my way to find some coffee," he said. "I think I'll be needing it."

Clay grimaced. "If you drink the coffee in this place, you'll be needing a stomach pump." He turned to Mary Jane. "We'll take over with Jimmy, now," he said. "Then Becca's going over to pick up Christina at Shannon's house. Why don't you go with Garrett and get something to eat?"

"Oh, well, I don't…" Her words stumbled over each other as she looked at the three people before her. What could she say that would sound reasonable?

"Don't tell me my dad's been so rough on you over the years that you'd refuse to let me buy you a sandwich and a cup of coffee," Garret said.

Becca and Clay were staring at her as if they couldn't believe that was the reason behind her reluctance. It wasn't, but she couldn't tell them the truth, that she didn't want to be around him because she was weighed down by regret and guilt from the past…

"Of course not," she said, pressing her damp palms together in front of her. She gave the three of them a bright smile that had Becca's brows drawing together. Mary Jane wished she was better at hiding her feelings. "I'd like to get something to eat. Let me grab my purse." She slipped quietly back into Jimmy's room. Becca and Clay said good-bye to Garrett and followed hot on her heels.

"Mom? Is something wrong?" Becca asked. She gave a quick glance at her sleeping son and lowered her voice. "You look worried." She nodded toward the bed. "Jimmy's going to be okay."

Mary Jane snagged her shoulder bag from the

back of the chair beside the bed. "Of course he is. It's only that I'm a little tired. It's been a busy day, what with pulling cows out of mud and having a grandson with a broken arm," she answered evasively.

Becca and Clay exchanged the kind of glance she and Hal had once shared. It said, "We'll talk about this later. In private."

"If you say so," Becca responded. "Thanks for staying with Jimmy."

Nodding, Mary Jane turned toward the door and took a deep breath. Sometimes it was murder having a step-daughter who was also her best friend. She had absolutely *no* secrets from her. Reminding herself to be more cautious from now on, she rejoined Garrett in the corridor.

He was leaning against the wall, his arms folded across his chest and his eyes studying the beige and brown tile. His feet were crossed at the ankle, his face brooding and exhausted. Mary Jane paused. How many times had she seen him stand in exactly that pose? With that solemn, intense look of deep concern on his face? Dozens at least. It shook her to realize she remembered that about him.

She felt a surge of pity. She knew what it was like to pace these halls waiting for word about someone she loved. It must be even worse waiting for word on someone like Gus, who had made himself nearly impossible to love. No doubt, Garrett was trying to come to terms with his feelings for his father.

"Do the nurses know where to find you if you're needed?" she asked in a gentle tone as she stepped up beside him.

Garrett gave her a distracted glance. "Yes. They'll call me when Frank's made his diagnosis."

Mary Jane nodded, fought down the inappropriate urge to take his hand in a comforting grip, and led the way to the cafeteria. The room was deserted. They went through the line and got their coffee and sandwiches, which Garrett paid for with a faint smile. "For old time's sake," he said as they stepped to a table that looked out over the hospital's small rose garden. "You'd never let me spend much money on you."

"We had to hide from your father," she pointed out before she stopped to think. "So we couldn't go many places where we *could* spend much...." Stricken, she stared up at him, noting the way his jaw had gone stiff, his eyes cool. "I'm sorry," she whispered. "I shouldn't have said that." Grief, what had come over her? She was *never* rude and certainly never in a situation like this. Shakily, she sat and wrapped her hands around her coffee mug, unable to meet his eyes.

"No need to apologize," he said, lifting his cup and sipping the dark brew. "It's true. All that running and hiding from him must have gotten old. Is that why you were dating Hal at the same time?"

Mary Jane's head snapped up. "I wasn't," she denied.

His expression told her he didn't believe her. His brow lifted skeptically, but his eyes were watchful as he said, "It's understandable, I guess. After all, there was no one to say you shouldn't, or couldn't date Hal. You and I weren't engaged or anything, and Hal must have been attractive to you with his

stable life, his own ranch. Those things were more
than you'd ever had before.''

*Not to mention a house desperately in need of a
woman's touch, a six-year-old daughter, a mortgage
that nearly sank them every year for the first ten
years of their marriage and more hard work than
two people could finish in a lifetime.* Mary Jane
stared at him, appalled that he thought she'd been
dating him and Hal at the same time. Did he think
she'd chosen the man who could offer her more? In
a way, she had, but only because she had been pregnant with Garrett's baby and he'd made it clear he
wanted nothing more to do with her.

The letter postmarked at the army base where
he'd been in basic training, had told her not to write
to him, that this was the end of things between them.

Foolish girl that she was, she'd still tried to contact him. Against his wishes, she'd written to him
again, even tried to call him. She'd been absolutely
convinced that if he knew she was pregnant, he
would insist on marriage. Of course, she'd been
wrong. He hadn't even answered her letters. Years
later, she'd discovered that she could have contacted
him through his commanding officer, but that was
something she hadn't known as a scared eighteen-
year-old.

Mary Jane lifted her chin, aware that she'd been
silent too long. There were certain things she had to
continue to keep to herself—Shannon being the
most important one—but she fully intended to set
him straight about a few others.

''Yes,'' she answered coolly. ''My no-account
white trash family didn't go in much for stability,
home and family or hard work. As my big brother

Dave said, our relatives preferred to remain job-less.''

"So Hal offered you a better deal.''

Her lips tight, she said, "The only one I wanted. Hal was a wonderful, decent man who promised me a good life, and he delivered on that promise.''

"Whereas, I had promised you nothing," Garrett said, his voice dark as if he was probing into corners best left in obscurity.

"As you say," Mary Jane agreed. "You had promised me nothing." And took everything, she thought, fighting bitterness. Her hands shook as she lifted the cup to her lips, and took a sip of coffee. Taking a breath, she reminded herself that she'd been through worse things. She could handle this. Her gaze came up to meet his. "Do you really want to talk about this right now? This has been a terrible day for you. Why dredge up the past?''

Garrett's deep-set eyes held hers for a long moment as if he wanted to deny it. As if he was so strong and macho he could handle the impossible situation with his father as well as touchy conversations with her. "Maybe I'm feeling nostalgic," he answered, but then he changed the subject, asking about people they'd known in high school, the changes that had taken place in Tarrant over the years, and the struggling ranching industry.

Mary Jane relaxed a bit as she talked, but their conversation simmered in the back of her mind. If she had any doubts that he wasn't finished with the subject, Garrett dispelled them when the nurse tracked him down to tell him that Dr. Kress had finished his examination and would see him now.

He nodded to the nurse and stood. "I'll be seeing you, Mary Jane. We still have lots to discuss."

Dread settled inside her and dried up any response she might have fabricated. As she watched him leave, she had the sinking feeling that he spoke the truth. They would finish their conversation and neither of them would like the outcome.

Gus Blackhawk suffered another massive stroke and died that night, never having regained consciousness. Mary Jane learned that Garrett had spent the night by his father's bedside, watching over the man who had driven him away so many years before.

She went about her work the next day, overcome with sadness. She called the Blackhawk ranch to express her condolences and to offer her help, but Garrett was in town making funeral arrangements and Ruth Chandliss said that little help would be needed. After all, there would be no relatives coming in for the funeral. Garrett was the only family Gus had possessed. There would be a graveside service in a few days and the details would be in the local paper.

Depressed, and yet guiltily relieved that her lifetime of struggles with her difficult neighbor were over, Mary Jane hung up, wishing she had someone to talk this over with. The only one who knew all the details was her brother, Dave, and he had recently moved to Denver. For the first time in two years, she missed Hal as if his death was a fresh loss. Knowing she couldn't discuss this with anyone made her feel bereft and alone, emotions she usually kept herself too busy to experience.

Giving in to the need to talk to someone, she called Becca to ask about Jimmy.

"He's okay, Mom," Becca answered gaily. "He was allowed to come home this morning and he's milking this broken arm situation for all it's worth. Right now, he's playing with the toys Mr. Blackhawk sent him."

A picture of Gus flashed through Mary Jane's mind, but then she realized with a jolt that he wasn't the one Becca meant. *"Garrett?"* she asked. *"Garrett* sent Jimmy some toys?"

"Yes. Expensive ones from the hospital gift shop. In fact, he probably spent so much money on these, the hospital's ladies' auxiliary will build a wing with his name on it. I didn't know the two of you were such good friends that he would take time from being with his father to do something like this for your grandson."

Mary Jane's breath clogged in her throat. Her gaze lifted to the window and she stared blindly in the direction of the Blackhawk ranch. Or maybe he was feeling guilty for what he'd said to her at the hospital. "I...I didn't know that we were, either, Becca. He was only being kind."

"*Very* kind. It surprised me, but you've always said he's nothing like his father." Her voice dropped. "That poor, sad old man."

"Yes, yes, he was," Mary Jane agreed. "I'm glad Jimmy's okay. I'll talk to you later. I've got things to do." Like try to figure out why Garrett would have done such a thing. Was it a signal to her that she needed to keep him in mind? As if she could forget him! Was it a promise that he wouldn't forget that they still had things to discuss?

Maybe. Either way, he'd insured she wouldn't forget about him. In fact, he'd made his presence known throughout her family. Jimmy would talk endlessly about the toys and the man who had given them to him, though she doubted the two of them had met. Brittnie would hear about it, and so would Shannon.

Mary Jane stopped and closed her eyes as she offered up a desperate plea. She didn't want Shannon to be aware of Garrett, to question her about him. She wasn't ready to answer the inevitable questions.

She poured herself a glass of water, took a sip, then another, and she finally began to calm down. Maybe she was overreacting.

What was she so worried about, anyway? Garrett wasn't going to be around very long. He would take care of the funeral arrangements and go back to Albuquerque. That's where his life was, his business. No doubt, he would sell the Blackhawk ranch, or lease it out. The place had few happy memories for him. There was very little chance that Garrett and Shannon would ever meet.

Relieved by this conclusion, Mary Jane headed into her office to do some paperwork. She was panicking over nothing. This whole thing was going to blow over and life would return to normal, exactly as it had been before she'd made that fateful phone call to Garrett.

Satisfied with her reasoning, Mary Jane buried herself in work and ignored the little voice that said she was fooling herself.

# CHAPTER THREE

"MOM, YOU'RE GOING OVER to the house after the graveside service, aren't you?"

Mary Jane turned and stared at Becca, then at her other two daughters. She had only attended the funeral out of courtesy, but her daughters had insisted on accompanying her. She should have expected it since they had been the ones encouraging her to call Garrett and tell him how sick Gus was. Even their husbands had come, though only Shannon's husband, Luke Farraday, had known Gus.

When they had arrived at the cemetery, Mary Jane had purposely stood back in hopes of keeping Shannon out of Garrett's direct line of sight. So far, it had worked, and if her family thought her behavior was strange, they kept their opinions to themselves and respected her wishes. That was the advantage of being the matriarch of her little clan, she thought ironically. They did as she asked. She assured herself firmly that she was far too young for the term *matriarch*.

Their small group stood at the edge of the gathering of people who had come to see Gus Blackhawk find the peace he'd never known in life. The September wind blew across the dry ground, setting dust devils dancing through what remained of the summer grass. When the service ended, the other mourners spoke to Garrett, then moved toward their cars. Garrett stood beside the still-open grave and spoke quietly to the minister who had led the service.

She was struck by how incredibly handsome he was in the beautifully tailored black suit that emphasized the darkness of his hair and the width of his shoulders. Inanely, she wondered if he had flown back to his home for the suit. The fit was too perfect for him to have bought it off the rack, especially anywhere in Tarrant. It gave him a tall and solid presence as he bent his head to speak to the minister, a slight, quiet man.

The minister was a good pastor to the small community church, but he was new in the area and couldn't possibly have known that his invitation at the end of the service for the mourners to say a few words about the deceased would be met with resounding silence. Garrett had quickly smoothed it over by stepping forward and inviting everyone back to the house for refreshments.

"I hadn't really planned on it, Becca," she answered, returning to her daughter's question. "I really need to get straight back home. There's lots of work to do, and…."

"But, Mom," Shannon broke in, her deep-blue eyes wide with surprise. "We were his neighbors, and while he wasn't very nice to us, Dad would have expected us to go pay our respects."

"That's right," Brittnie and Becca chimed in together.

Mary Jane stared at them in dismay. They were right, of course. They should go to the house, in order to show that Gus's meanness to them all those years was forgiven. She would have to risk the possibility of Shannon and Garrett meeting face to face.

After a lifetime of telling them that neighbors helped neighbors, watched out for each other, forgave and forgot, she couldn't suddenly say that she and their father had lied to them all those years, that common courtesy didn't apply in this case.

Her heart sinking, she nodded. "You're right. We'll go for a little while." Even that was strange, because she usually stayed to help clean up after the guests had left. Surely, she could get out of that, without completely ruining her reputation in the community?

As soon as they saw Garrett shake hands with the minister and leave the cemetery, her family climbed into their cars and made the short drive to the Blackhawk ranch. Mary Jane rode with Shannon and Luke, and, as they made the turn into the ranch road, she heard Shannon gasp in dismay. A range-management specialist, Shannon could see that the place had been sadly neglected.

"I'd heard about this," she said quietly. "But I didn't know how bad it was. I wonder if Mr. Blackhawk would let us start working here, bringing it back before it's ruined forever." She had recently been put in charge of the natural resources office and was very enthusiastic about her job.

"If anyone can do it, you can," Luke answered with a hint of a lop-sided grin. "After all, you did it with my place. *Our* place," he corrected himself.

"Garrett will probably sell it," Mary Jane broke in quickly. "He's got his own ranch and business in Albuquerque and he'll be going back there." And the sooner the better, she added silently.

Shannon gave her a quick look, no doubt wondering about the sharpness of her tone. Mary Jane glanced away, unable to think of anything else to say. She just wanted to get this day over, to hurry Shannon away, to shield her from learning the truth, but they were headed straight toward it.

They pulled up in front of the ranch house which retained its sad, empty look even though there were a dozen cars parked in the yard. There was simply no way to make a house look approachable when so much unhappiness had taken place inside. She took a deep breath and stepped from the car when Luke held out his hand for her.

Once inside, she was gratified to see that the living room was crowded and that Garrett wasn't in sight. In spite of her desire to escape as quickly as possible, when Mary Jane saw that Ruth Chandliss was setting up a buffet supper in the dining room, she hurried to help, her daughters right behind her.

The housekeeper looked up with a vague smile. She was well into her seventies and had worked here for forty years. As difficult as it must have been to work for Gus Blackhawk, she hadn't wanted to retire. Mary Jane wondered what she would do now that her employer was dead.

Within a few minutes, they had the food set out. While Ruth was moving through the crowd quietly telling people to help themselves, Mary Jane hurried into the kitchen for more silverware.

Ruth had it laid out neatly on the table, but before Mary Jane could scoop it up, she heard a noise coming from the back porch. Curious, she stepped out there to see Garrett standing by the large, upright freezer. He had a plastic bag of ice in each hand which he lifted onto the counter. When he saw her, he announced in a harsh tone, ''We're having punch. We're using my mother's sterling silver punchbowl. It hasn't been out of its box since she died.''

Mary Jane's eyes widened. He had taken off his jacket and rolled up his sleeves, exhibiting powerful forearms. He'd been a tall, wiry boy. When had he become so...solid? She snapped her mind back to the subject at hand and blurted, ''Won't it be tarnished?''

Garrett swung around and she fell back a step at the fierce light in his eyes. ''Tarnished?''

The hardness in his face had her taking another half-step back. ''That...that's what happens to sterling silver, you know, especially after it's been sitting for more than forty years.''

Garrett stared at her for a second, then he shook his head and one corner of his mouth kicked up in annoyance. ''I didn't even think of that. I guess we won't use it. I saw all the things that have been sitting around, unused, for so long, and thought, 'Well, why not?'''

Compassion washed over her. There must be many things in this house that had been as neglected as the punchbowl. She gave him a soft smile. ''No one will mind, Garrett. They're not here to see your mother's punch bowl. They're here out of respect for you.''

''For me? They don't even know me anymore.''

''You're wrong. The people in this valley have kept track of you and all your accomplishments.''

His dark eyes searched her face. ''And are you one of them, Mary Jane? Have you kept track of my accomplishments?''

She didn't like the look in his eyes, or the question he was asking her. "I'm one of the people in this valley, aren't I?" she answered evasively.

"You sure are," he said in a grim tone. "You'll never leave here, will you?"

Now what? She stared at him. "It's my home."

"Then I guess it's a good thing my father didn't succeed in driving you off your place. Instead, he's the one who's gone," he said in a quietly taunting voice, then stepped closer. "Are you here to make sure the old man is dead?"

"Certainly not," she said on an outraged gasp, lifting her chin to meet his gaze as he towered over her.

"You're not rejoicing that your troubles are over? Ruth has told me how often he called the sheriff on you and your family over the years. Aren't you glad that you don't have to worry about that anymore? About him trying to run the lives of everyone in this valley?"

Appalled, Mary Jane stared at him. The bitterness in his voice shook her and she couldn't quite decide if it was directed at his dead father or at her. "Garrett, your father died a lonely and unhappy man. I would never rejoice in that."

Garrett studied her expression for a minute, then he shook his head. "Hell," he growled, running a hand over his eyes. "I know you wouldn't. I'm sorry. I..."

Reaching up, she laid her hand on his arm. "It's okay, Garrett. His problems weren't your fault, or your responsibility. He chose to be the way he was, but it's all right for you to grieve for the man he should have been, the one you would have wanted him to be."

Garrett looked down at her hand as it rested on his arm. Slowly, he lifted his own hand and covered hers, holding her in place. "You're right," he said, his voice low and quiet. "I know that, but I have to keep reminding myself of it. There was so much unsaid between us…and now it never will be."

He lifted his head and stared into her eyes. For a second, Mary Jane wondered if he was talking about himself and his father, or the two of them. She became aware of his hand entrapping hers against the warm, vital flesh of his arm.

Her breath went thready in her chest, squeezing out through her throat in a soft wheeze. Garrett leaned down to her, his eyes fixed on hers as if daring her to step back, move away. Run.

Neither of them moved or said a word. It was as if they were challenging each other to break away first, or to come closer.

*This is wrong.* Mary Jane's eyes were wide. *This is an insane thing to do in this house of mourning.* But she didn't move.

Garrett's hand finally shifted. His palm traveled upwards in a smooth, sliding motion that made the black silk of her sleeve whisper in a sensual invitation. His fingers wrapped around her shoulder and drew her forward. Neither of them blinked. She didn't try to pull away.

Her heart was pounding in her throat, then up into her ears. Heat rushed up her neck and throat, scorching her. She moaned in distress.

The sound had Garrett's lips twisting up as if he liked that reaction. Then his mouth was on hers.

Heat and lightning, wrapped in a fist of dark needs rolled over her. Her body bucked, her breath jerked in, bringing his scent, and the memories with it. This wasn't the boy she'd known all those years ago. This was the man that boy had become, and yet he tasted, felt the same.

With a low groan, Garrett brought his arms down to wrap around her waist. He urged her up, against his hard, strong body as he held her close. Her hands shot up to steady herself against his broad shoulders, then she felt the solid presence of his body. Her hands clenched against his crisp white shirt. She hesitated only a second before circling his neck and plunging her fingers eagerly into his hair.

The taste of him was so familiar, yet so long-denied. Hot, sweet, salty, she couldn't decide. She leaned closer and came up on her toes, seeking more of it.

Garrett's mouth ravaged hers with long, hard kisses that stopped her breath and heated her blood. His arms were strong, holding her against him in a powerful grip.

It had been so long. So long since a strong, healthy man had held her. Years since Hal had been well and strong, holding her like this.... Hal. Shannon.

As if someone had dumped one of the bags of ice over her head, Mary Jane came swiftly and suddenly to her senses. She wrenched herself from his arms and stumbled away from him until she was stopped by the freezer. The back of her hand came up to cover her mouth and her shocked, shamed eyes stared at him.

"You...you shouldn't. We..." she corrected herself, realizing that part of the responsibility was hers. Her hand fell away, she took a breath, composed herself, and clasped her hands in front of her. "We shouldn't do this. It's not the time or the place."

Garrett was getting his ragged breathing under control much more quickly than she was. His eyes were sharp as they studied her face. "There was a time when you wouldn't have cared where or when I kissed you."

"I hope I've matured a little since then and that you have, too." She clutched her fingers together tightly. She was shaking deep inside and it was going to start breaking to the outside any second now, showing him just how affected she was.

"Maybe I have and maybe I haven't, and maybe there are some things a man never outgrows," he said. "I didn't expect this, and neither did you, but it's here between us now, and…"

"Mom, we need the silverware, and… Mom?"

Shannon's voice! Alarmed, Mary Jane shot away from the freezer and dashed from the porch. She caught a glimpse of Garrett's startled face as she rushed past, but she didn't pause. Her only thought was to get away, to get Shannon away, as panicked and unreasonable as that might seem.

She hurried into the kitchen where the wild look in her eyes, her disheveled hair and swollen lips had Shannon staring in amazement. "Mom? Are you okay?"

"Yes, of course," she answered, her voice reedy and breathless. She stopped, smoothed her hair and looked around the unfamiliar kitchen. "I came in here to… Here," she said, snatching up the silverware that Ruth had left on the table. "Let's take this in." She made a grab for Shannon's arm, but her

daughter pulled away as her gaze shot to the door
leading from the porch.

Fear clutched at her throat and she turned to face
Garrett who was striding into the room, the bags of
ice dangling from his hands. He set them in the sink.
His voice was calm and controlled when he asked,
"Is this one of your daughters, Mary Jane?"

Her mouth was so dry she couldn't talk. She could
only stare with a sense of sick inevitability as
Shannon moved across the room, her hand out-
stretched. Why had she taught her children such
good manners, Mary Jane wondered hysterically.
Why hadn't she taught them to turn and run when
they met a stranger?

"How do you do, Mr. Blackhawk?" she said.
"I'm Shannon Farraday. I guess you could say I'm
a neighbor twice over. As you know, I grew up on
the Running K and now my husband and I own the
Crescent Ranch."

Garrett's head tilted up. "Oh, yes, my dad owned
it for many years." His eyes slid to Mary Jane's
stricken face. She knew he was recalling that Gus
had bought it for Garrett, dangling it in front of him
like a carrot before a donkey, saying that he could
have it for his own when he dumped Mary Jane.

She'd always thought it was strange that though
he had, indeed, dumped her, he'd never taken over
the Crescent Ranch. No doubt there were other
strings that Gus had attached.

These reflections swept through her mind in a
flash, then she focused on her tall, lovely daughter
standing beside her biological father. *My God.* Mary
Jane swallowed a gasp of dismay. *Can't they see the*

*resemblance of black hair, blue eyes, high cheek-
bones, squarely stubborn chin?*

Apparently they couldn't. Shannon told Garrett
how sorry she was for his loss, he nodded his ac-
knowledgment, and the two of them turned back to
their tasks.

Mary Jane almost sank to her knees in fervent
relief. The moment she had dreaded for so long had
happened. It was over, and the sky hadn't fallen on
her.

The door burst open again and Ruth marched in.
"What is this?" she asked, clapping her hands onto
her hips. "Some kind of black hole in space? People
disappear looking for ice and silverware and are
never seen again."

The three in the kitchen jumped in surprise.
Shannon hurried out with the silverware, and Mary
Jane followed, leaving Ruth and Garrett to bring the
ice.

Even though she desperately wanted to leave,
Mary Jane knew she would be needed. When her
daughters and their husbands said their good-byes
and left, she told them she would catch a ride home
with another neighbor. She was eager to have them
gone and once they were, she quickly took herself
out of Garrett's line of sight, circulating on the far
side of the room, talking to people she hadn't seen
in a while. As she made her rounds, spoke to friends,
helped Ruth, and avoided making eye contact with
Garrett, her mind was in a whirl.

What had she been *thinking?* Kissing Garrett as
if she would have liked to crawl right inside his
skin? Kissing Garrett at all? Her behavior was so

wildly inappropriate and out of character, she couldn't make sense of it.

She could only conclude that it had been some combination of curiosity and insanity on her part, as well as the desires of a woman who obviously needed to get out more and develop a social life!

As to Garrett's motivations, perhaps he was curious, as well. Maybe he was regretting the way he'd taunted her about Gus.

Several times, she felt Garrett's attention on her and she looked up to meet his eyes. He didn't seem to be suffering any of the pangs of conscience she was experiencing. He watched her with thoughtful regard as if he was trying to determine exactly what was going on in her mind.

The sole thing in her mind right now was the keen hope that this day would end soon.

When the crowd thinned out, Mary Jane helped Ruth put things away, gave her friend a departing hug, then rushed out to the front porch to see if she could catch a ride with someone.

She saw with relief that Pete Minton was shaking hands with Garrett in preparation for leaving. Pete's wife, Sheryl was already in the car. Mary Jane hurried up to him. "Pete, can I catch a ride with you?" she asked breathlessly. "I rode over with my family, but they all had to leave and get back to work."

Her neighbor nodded, then settled his hat on his bald head. "Sure, Mary Jane. We were just about…"

"I'll take you home," Garrett broke in. His dark, steady gaze held hers.

She smiled, despite the stiffness of her lips, and lifted her hand in a lightly dismissive gesture. "Really, that's not necessary. Pete goes right by my place, and..."

"I said I'll take you home." He gave Pete's hand another swift shake. "It's good to see you again, buddy."

Pete nodded and strode to his car as Mary Jane turned to Garrett. "You don't have to put yourself out for me."

One of his dark brows lifted and she saw a hint of deviltry in his eyes. "Why not? You put yourself out for me."

Her spine stiffened.

"By helping Ruth, I mean. Thanks. I'll go get my keys," he said, turning away. "I'll be right back."

Frustrated, she paced the porch while she waited for him to return, her steps short and choppy with irritation. She was tempted to walk as it was only one mile from the driveway of the Blackhawk ranch to the road leading to the Running K, but she knew Garrett would insist on picking her up, so she might as well wait. Besides, she wasn't accustomed to wearing high heels and these things would cripple her if she walked far in them.

He was back within a few minutes, jingling a set of keys in his hand. "It's in the garage," he said, tilting his head toward the roomy structure at the north end of the house.

"Thank you," she said, and stalked down the stairs. He followed her, not even bothering to keep up.

She knew she was being ungracious, but she couldn't seem to help it. She felt disconcerted, embarrassed, thrown off-kilter. There was no explanation for the craziness that had overtaken her when she had kissed him. Mrs. Kelleher, the upstanding citizen, pillar of the community, mother of three, grandmother of two, didn't *do* things like that, especially not with someone she so strongly wanted to avoid.

Her heart gave a sad, lonely kick. She didn't do those things with anyone.

Garrett strode around her and lifted the big, creaking door of the garage. As light flooded in, Mary Jane walked toward the old truck Gus had always driven, thinking sadly how he would have hated knowing she was riding in it. She glanced around at the tools and loose car parts stacked on shelves and spilling across the floor, then caught sight of Garrett's dismayed face as he held the truck door open for her.

"Will you be selling the ranch?" she asked. "And clearing out the house?"

He cast her a sideways glance as if he'd caught the note of hope in her tone. "Yes. There's no need to keep it. My life and business are in Albuquerque."

"Oh, it only makes sense for you to do that," Mary Jane said, trying to sort through the mixture of relief and disappointment she was feeling. She *wanted* him to return to his home and business, didn't she? She didn't want him and Shannon to come face to face again. Their one meeting had nearly stopped her heart—what little of her heart had still been functioning after the kiss they had shared.

Now *that* was something that certainly didn't need to be repeated.

She was grateful when they pulled into her own driveway. "No need to get out," she said brightly.

"Thanks for bringing me home." She turned her head and saw that he was giving her an inquiring look as he climbed out. He was opening her door for her before she knew it, then reaching and taking her hand to help her out.

"You've got a nice place here, Mary Jane," he said, taking a long, slow look at the neatly kept fences, the barn with the fresh coat of paint she and her sons-in-law had applied the month before, and the few fat yearlings that grazed close to the corral.

"Thank you." Pride showed in her face as she looked around. "Hal and I worked hard to build it up."

Garrett closed the car door and leaned against it. He crossed his arms over his chest as he regarded her. "Was he a good husband to you, Mary Jane?"

They'd had this conversation before and she wasn't anxious to return to it. "Of course. The best."

"But he's gone now, has been for several years."

She edged away from him, not liking where this was heading.

"And my father is dead, so now everything's changed for me, too."

"What do you mean?"

"I mean what I was trying to tell you a while ago, that there is still something between us. It didn't die twenty-eight years ago, it didn't die even when you were married, even though my father made things impossible for you, for *both* of us."

Against all reason, a spark of hope fluttered into her throat. She pushed it away ruthlessly. "The past is dead and buried, Garrett, and that's the way it should stay."

"That's what you think." He stepped forward suddenly and took her chin in his hand. For an instant, she feared he was going to kiss her again, but he didn't. Instead, he looked into her eyes and said, "I can't figure out exactly what it is you're afraid of."

Panic blossomed in her eyes. "I…I'm not afraid of anything," she bluffed.

He answered with a derisive snort. "Yes, you are." He leaned forward and grazed a light kiss over her forehead. "And I promise you, I'm going to find out what it is."

Releasing her, Garrett stepped away, climbed back into the truck and drove off, leaving Mary Jane to grip the handrail by the porch steps to support her as she stared after him in distress. He had no right, she thought, suddenly furious. He had no right to come in and upset her life like this. He'd made it clear many years ago that he wanted nothing to do with her. He wasn't going to suddenly change his mind now. She wouldn't let him interfere in her life and that of her family.

The next time she saw him she would make that very clear. He thought he was going to have things his way, but he wasn't. What had been between them was long over and she wasn't going to let her life be disrupted by another member of the Blackhawk family.

Why didn't he just spend his spare time letting bulls run loose in china shops? Garrett thought with distaste as he drove away from the Running K. They would have almost as much finesse as he did. He glanced in the rear-view mirror and saw Mary Jane scurrying into her house. In spite of the chug of the truck's engine, he could almost hear the slap of the screen door closing behind her.

He turned his attention to his driving. For a man who thought he knew himself pretty well, he couldn't have said why he'd kissed Mary Jane the way he had. For old times' sake, maybe? Curiosity? Both of those, as well as needs he'd thought had died out long ago. He'd been sure they'd died out because he had ruthlessly tried to kill them.

It was a hell of a thing to find out after all this time that he'd failed. He wanted her, it was that simple. And to her mind, that impossible.

Why did it panic her? he wondered. Was she still so much in love with her husband that she couldn't look at another man? If so, why had she responded to him with enough force and eagerness to blow the top of his head off?

If she was still in love with her late husband, Hal was lucky. Garrett found himself in the unhappy position of envying a dead man. What kind of pitiful specimen did that make him?

He turned into the rutted driveway leading to his father's place. *His* place now, he corrected himself, looking around with a sinking feeling. His grief over his father's death, the guilty feeling that their final argument had brought it on, and the miserable way things had ended between them were all mixed with distress at the way the old man had let things run down.

Garrett had offered more than once to help out, to hire some hands, pay them top dollar to get them to stay. Gus wouldn't hear of it, had cut him off with a sharp retort when he'd even mentioned it.

Offering help had been pointless, anyway, Garrett thought ruefully. Gus's tiresome demands and suspicious nature would have driven away any hands within a few days.

Garrett knew he should have pushed harder, but he'd had no idea the place was in such bad shape. No doubt, Ruth would have told him if she hadn't feared losing her job. Garrett wondered if Gus had ever appreciated Ruth's loyalty.

It would take weeks to get the ranch into shape to sell and the house and barn were full of things he needed to sort. Too bad it was against the law to simply throw on some gasoline, light a match, and run.

Of course, Ruth would help him. He intended to keep her on the payroll, and she'd be happy to keep busy by going through and sorting some of the things Gus had never let her touch during his lifetime, including the items that had belonged to Garrett's mother. As far as he knew, they were still boxed away in the attic.

That meant he'd be back in Tarrant in a few weeks. Maybe he'd even spend part of the Christmas holidays here. It would be a change from his place in Albuquerque, or the skiing vacations he sometimes took in Aspen.

Best of all, he could see Mary Jane again, try to find out exactly why they were still so attracted to each other, and why she wanted to fight it so hard.

That idea alone was enough to make him eager for the holidays to arrive. He grinned fleetingly as he pulled up in front of the house and stopped. He wondered if he could wangle an invitation to Christmas dinner out of Mary Jane.

# CHAPTER FOUR

"WHAT THE *hell* are you doing?"

When the gruff voice crackled behind her, Mary Jane started in surprise and let go of the hay bale she'd been wrestling out of the back of her pickup. It thumped to the ground, barely missing her toes and startling the cattle nearest her. They lumbered back, bawling.

She whirled around and yelled, "Feeding cattle, obviously! Don't you know not to sneak up…. Oh, Garrett." Her eyes widened as she looked up at him, seated on the back of the biggest, blackest stallion she had ever seen. He was dressed in black, too, from his jeans and boots to the winter shearling jacket that kept out the chill of the November afternoon.

Horse and rider together were a big, powerful force to be reckoned with.

Her heart thudded in her chest. He looked like the essence of every B-movie western bad guy ever filmed. His blue eyes examined her from her own scuffed boots and worn jeans to Hal's heavy barn jacket, which she wore over a long-sleeved T-shirt and a flannel shirt that had long since seen better days.

"Feeding cattle by yourself?" Garrett asked, throwing his leg over the stallion's back and dropping lightly to the ground. He gathered the reins and tied them to a post of the fence that separated her

57

land from his. The stallion tossed his head, ignored
the humans, and set to grazing on the drying grass
within reach.

"That's right," she said, resettling her hat and
jerking up her gloves. She grabbed for the next bale.

Garrett's hands rested lightly at his hips as he
glanced around at the wide open fields. "Don't you
have anyone to help you?"

She lifted her chin, not liking his tone, or his in-
ference that she didn't have enough sense to know
how to do this on her own. "Not at the moment, no.
My hired man went to Durango for a few days. On
business," she added in a no-nonsense tone.

The truth was that the man who'd been working
for her had gone to the nearby city for the weekend
and ended up in jail after a three-day drinking binge.
She wasn't going to bail him out, and she wasn't
going to tell Garrett about it, either.

"I'll help you," Garrett said, stepping up on his
side of the fence, and looking for a way across.

She lifted her chin, and gave him a fierce look
that would have had most people backing down.
"No thanks, I can handle it." Darn, why had this
happened? she wondered. Where had he come from?
She hadn't even known he was back in Tarrant.

By the beginning of November, she had completely forgotten that Garrett was going to be returning to the valley, or so she told herself. She went
on as she always had, doing her chores, taking care
of the business of ranching, seeing her children often, and occasionally baby-sitting for her grandchildren.

When she had thought about Garrett over the past
few weeks, it was with a mixture of surprise and

irritation. Surprise because he had kissed her and irritation because she'd let him and she'd liked it. The whole episode was one she had shoved off to one corner of her mind and sealed with a label—Mistakes Not To Be Repeated. She'd promised herself she wouldn't remove that label.

"No need to trouble yourself," she said briskly. "And, besides, you're on the wrong side of the fence to help me. Thanks all the same."

"That's easily remedied," he said, swinging into the saddle, urging his mount around and starting off in the opposite direction. When they'd cantered several yards, he stopped, leaned over the horse's head and whispered into the animal's ear.

It took Mary Jane a full ten seconds to realize what he was going to do. When she did, she leaped onto the truck's running board, then scrambled into the truck bed. "Garrett," she shouted, throwing out her hands. "No!"

He ignored her, spurring the stallion into a gallop, and then into a flat-out run. The powerful animal's hooves pounded the ground as he raced for the fence. Garrett's face was set with intensity and excitement as he pushed the horse onward. Before Mary Jane could shout another protest, horse and rider were up, then over the fence, clearing it with inches to spare. When they landed, he leaned over and patted the stallion's neck then pulled the reins around so they trotted in a big circle and stopped beside the truck.

He looked up at her and grinned, his eyes sparkling with excitement. "At your service, ma'am," he said.

Mary Jane clapped a hand to her pounding heart,

and gasped out, "Aren't you a little old for that kind of thing?"

"You're only as old as you feel."

"Then you must be about sixteen, which is how old you were the first time I ever saw you pull that trick. I was afraid you were going to break your neck and the horse's, too."

"But I didn't," he said, taking off his hat and using it to make a sweeping bow. "And I'm still alive to tell the tale."

"And to scare the daylights out of me," she muttered darkly as she climbed out of the truck bed and returned to work. Cattle crowded in close as she snagged wire cutters out of her back pocket, cut the wire and began distributing the hay.

"I'm touched that you were worried," he said, then patted his horse's neck. "And so is Renegade."

She didn't respond as he swung out of the saddle. How could she have forgotten that he liked to take chances? That hadn't changed, probably would never change, no matter what his age.

When they'd first begun dating so many years ago in high school, she'd been attracted to his daredevil ways. She realized now that she'd been addicted to the chaos of a wild relationship because she'd grown up in a home ruled by the impulses of her alcoholic father. For Garrett, of course, the attraction had been in knowing he was going with someone his father could never accept; the girl from the wrong side of the tracks—if Tarrant had possessed any tracks. Their entire relationship had been based on all the wrong things—his need to show his father he couldn't be bossed around, and hers for someone to love her with the kind of unconditional love she'd craved. They had kept their dates a secret from almost everyone except her brother.

The sneaking around, secret meetings, midnight rides on horses Garrett spirited out of his father's corral, were all things that had fed her youthful need for drama.

Of course, a relationship like that was doomed to failure. It hadn't been built on respect, interests, or any of the things she'd shared with Hal. It had been a show-off, defy-their-families-and-backgrounds kind of connection.

And there had been lust. Hot, needful, raucous lust that neither of them had known how to handle. Everything about their time together had been wrong. Dave had tried to tell her that, but she'd been too besotted to listen.

She took a deep breath and calmed her pounding heart. Thank goodness she'd outgrown the crazy need for Garrett's brand of love, but too bad he still felt it was necessary to take chances. What she had told him was true. Years may have passed, but some things never changed.

She wished she could forget about feeding and go back home. There was plenty of work she could be doing in the barn or in the house, away from this cold wind, and Garrett's unwanted help. But that would be running away, something *she* had certainly outgrown. Besides, she was almost finished and once the two of them got to work, with Garrett pulling the bales out of the truck, her cutting the wire, and both of them scattering the hay, the cattle would be fed in no time.

Mary Jane made two more stops to feed the animals gathered around the stock-watering tanks and

Garrett rode along, dismounting to help her each time. She tried not to notice how good it felt to be working with a partner again, the way she and Hal had always worked together. She didn't know how she could be thinking such thoughts about him after the lecture she had given herself, but there it was.

Every tiny breeze brought a whiff of his scent; leather, tangy aftershave, a hint of honest male sweat, all the things she didn't want to notice but was helpless to avoid.

Really, it was too bad she didn't carry blinders in the truck so she could block out the sight of him. And maybe a giant clothespin to stick on her nose so she wouldn't smell him.

The thought struck her as funny, she lost her focus for a moment, and the wire cutters jabbed her thumb.

"Ouch!" She jerked back her hand and dropped the cutters.

"What's the matter?" Garrett demanded. "Are you hurt?"

She took off her glove and looked at the long red scrape along the pad of her thumb. "No. It's okay. Didn't even break the skin."

"Let me see." He took her hand in his. Mary Jane started to pull it away, but he said, "Stand still." As he examined it, she was struck by the contrast in their hands. They seemed to show equal amounts of wear—she even had calluses to match his—but she had more nicks, scrapes and scars.

"Are you up to date on your tetanus shots?"

She burst out laughing. "Are you kidding?' she asked, pointing to the damage she'd done over the years. "I always manage to injure myself with the sharp side of any iron bar, the business end of any blade, and the rustiest section of barbed wire. I *never* let my tetanus shot lapse.''

Garrett went very still, then lifted his head and looked into her eyes. ''You work too hard,'' he said.

Her smile faded and she tugged her glove back into place. ''Hard work's the only kind I know,'' she answered. ''So why don't we get back to it?''

Garrett's focus stayed on her for several more seconds, his eyes narrowed and assessing. Finally, he bent to pick up the wire cutters, handed them to her, and they returned to work.

When they had finished the feeding, she gratefully removed her heavy leather gloves and pulled some knit ones from her pocket. If she'd been alone, she would have smoothed on some of the hand cream she kept in the glove compartment, but that seemed a little too vain.

Tugging the gloves on to keep her hands warm, she looked up at Garrett and said, ''Thanks for your help. I'd better be getting home now.''

He ignored her dismissive tone. ''Got anything to drink in that truck of yours?'' he asked.

She stared at him. Of course he would be thirsty. They'd been working for more than an hour and he didn't seem to have so much as a canteen with him. ''Oh, yes. I have a water bottle and a cooler with some sodas. Sorry, I already drank all the hot coffee I brought with me.''

''Sodas, hm?'' he said. ''Not strawberry by any chance?''

She laughed unexpectedly and shook her head as her heart thudded against the base of her throat. Oh, the strawberry-flavored kisses they'd shared. She took a deep breath and tried for an easy, friendly smile. "You're the only person I ever knew who actually liked strawberry soda. You don't still drink it, do you?"

"Sure do. My house in Albuquerque has one refrigerator dedicated to nothing but strawberry soda. You'll have to come see it someday."

"Uh-huh," she said. The subject of his home wasn't one she wanted to delve into since she'd spent too much time thinking about it already. She walked to the truck, retrieved a can of cola for him and handed it over. "You'll have to make do with this."

"Thanks." He popped the tab, tilted his head back, and took a long swallow. As he did so, Mary Jane noticed the strong column of his neck, the rhythmic movement of his Adam's apple, the dark hair that curled over his collar, and remembered what it had been like when she'd kissed him the day of the funeral.

The memory still shamed her. The timing had been wrong, their actions disrespectful, yet it was the heat and the need that she remembered, and that added to her shame. Recalling it had heat and need building once again. Mary Jane looked away and forced a steadying breath.

Finished with the soda, Garrett crumpled the can in his fist and tossed it into her truck. "Thanks," he said. His eyes met hers as if he knew she'd been watching him and knew what she was thinking. "I'd better get back to the house. I wanted to take Renegade for a ride after the drive over from Albuquerque. He doesn't like the horse trailer."

Mary Jane dug her hands into the pockets of her

baggy coat. "Oh, well, some horses don't," she answered vaguely. She knew she was friendly and outgoing, but she wasn't good with small talk, especially with him. "Well, thanks again for the help, Garrett."

He scooped up Renegade's reins and prepared to mount. "Any time, Mary Jane. We're going to be neighbors for a while, so if ever you need anything, give me a call." His mocking tone told her he knew hell would freeze over before he received such a call.

Alarmed, she met his eyes. "For a while? Why?"

"Don't sound so panicked about it," he advised with an edge to his voice. "I've discovered that Gus's business affairs are in such a tangle, it'll take me months to straighten them out. I'll be splitting my time between here and Albuquerque until it's solved. That's why I brought Renegade with me," he said, bending down to pat the horse's neck. "So we could both get some exercise."

"Oh." She looked away, staring at the winter-brown grass, then in the distance, at a stand of trees that were dropping their yellowed leaves with each breath of wind. He was going to be staying at the Blackhawk ranch. Right here in Tarrant.

He wasn't like his father, holed up in his house for weeks at a time, then making a hurried trip to town. Garrett would be out and about among his friends and neighbors. She would be seeing him frequently. In her heart, joy and dread fought each other to a draw.

"I understand one of your daughters can help me with part of the problem with the ranch."

Shannon! Stark terror shot through her, and

brought her eyes up to his. Automatically, her shoulders squared and her fists came up to her sides. "Why?"

Garrett's eyes narrowed at her fiery reaction. *"Why?"* he asked incredulously.

"Yes. Why would you need her help? After all, you'll be selling the place, won't you? The new owner can do the improvements...."

"Selling the Blackhawk ranch is a long way off," Garrett said. "I've got lots of things to do first."

Panic set her heart bouncing and filled her mouth with a coppery tang. "Like what?"

He looked at her as if she'd lost her mind. "The house is full of old papers, mementos, historical things. I understand one of your daughters can sort and dispose of it for me."

*Brittnie then,* she thought, relieved. *Not Shannon.* That wasn't quite so bad, but it certainly wasn't good. "Ye...hes," she managed shakily. "My daughter Brittnie is a librarian and archivist, but she's very busy finishing up a project for her husband's family, sorting out things that belonged to his great-uncle, and..."

"And she wouldn't have time to even come out and discuss this with me?" Garrett asked on a harsh note. "I realize she's a professional and her time is valuable. I'll pay her a consulting fee."

"I'm sure that wouldn't be necessary," Mary Jane said, lifting her hand dismissively. "Besides, she lives in Durango, and..."

"And what?" he asked, puzzled. "It's forty-five minutes from here, not on the other side of the moon."

"She's really very busy."

"Are you her agent or something? Does she make all her arrangements, take all her jobs through you?"

"Well, no, of course not, but…"

"Then I'll talk to her in person," he said, scowling ferociously and clapping his hands onto his hips. "If she's an adult, a professional, a married woman, I doubt that she needs her mother's permission before speaking to me!"

"No, certainly not," Mary Jane answered. Pride in her daughters' accomplishments warred with the need to protect them.

"What is it with you?" he asked. "What do you think I am? The neighborhood kidnapper? Some kind of lecherous bastard out to hurt your little girl?" He turned suddenly and swung into the saddle, sending Renegade into a stirring dance as he snatched savagely at the reins. "I'm not," he said. "And the only one likely to hurt her is you with your crazy ideas."

Garrett spurred the horse around, made another of his heart-stopping fence jumps and raced away across the field.

Mary Jane slumped against the truck's tailgate and covered her eyes with a shaking hand. She couldn't handle this. She absolutely couldn't. Her fierce desire to protect Shannon and her other daughters was making her do and say things that were arousing his suspicions. She had to get a grip on this or it was going to explode in her face.

She lifted her head and stared after the horse and rider disappearing in the distance.

If it hadn't exploded already.

*    *    *

"Who would have thought he would have turned out to look like that? That's one handsome devil if I ever saw one." Millie Ferguson sighed as she finished bagging up the items Mary Jane had bought at the grocery store.

Mary Jane handed over the check to pay for her purchases. "Who?" she asked. "Look like what?"

Millie rolled her eyes. "Garrett, of course. And he looks like someone I wouldn't mind getting to know on a long, dark winter's night."

Mary Jane went still. Garrett. Was he here? Feigning nonchalance, she glanced around. "What would Don say?" she asked casually.

"My husband runs this store until ten o'clock every weeknight, remember?" the cashier said with a grin. "I'll tell him I'm at the ladies' sewing circle at the church."

"Until ten?" Mary Jane asked skeptically.

Millie sighed theatrically. "Making quilts for poor deserving souls in cold northern climates—and testing them," she said, wiggling her eyebrows.

Mary Jane smiled as she looked around the store again. Sure enough, right outside the plate glass windows, she could see Garrett. He'd stopped to talk to Don Ferguson, who was sweeping the front walk. The two of them had been friends in high school, had played football and basketball together. Mary Jane knew that because Garrett had told her, bragged about what a great team the two of them had made. The three of them had never talked together, though. In fact, she had never been included in that part of Garrett's life.

They'd never had a real date, gone to a movie, or out with his friends. That's why it had been easy to hide Shannon's true parentage. Except for her brother, few people had known she'd been involved with Garrett. Their time had been spent riding his horses, sitting in his car talking, or later, making love. She had been so crazy about him, she had refused to think he kept their relationship secret because he was ashamed of being with the daughter of the town drunk. She'd eventually seen the truth, but by then it had been too late.

The fault hadn't been his alone. She had wanted it kept quiet also, because she had known her father would have tried to force a marriage between her and Garrett. He'd always had an eye to the main chance and would have liked nothing more than finding a way to get his hands on some of Gus Blackhawk's money, even if it was as a buy-off to keep his daughter away from Gus's son.

"I'm new here," Millie said, handing Mary Jane her receipt. "Only been married to Don for twenty years, so I had no idea this town had ever produced men who looked like Garrett Blackhawk. Did you know him?"

"Yes." Mary Jane gathered up her bags of groceries. "I knew him." She didn't say any more, merely smiled at Millie, who was moving along to the next customer.

Against her better judgment, she had to agree with Millie and admit that Garrett looked darned good. He wore the same shearling-lined jacket he'd had on the last time they met. His Stetson, jeans, and boots were the normal winter wear for men in Tarrant, but they simply looked better on him with his wide shoulders, long legs, and solid stance. He stood with the sides of his jacket thrown back, his hands at his waist, his head tilted slightly so he could hear Don. Suddenly, he threw back his head and laughed, and Mary Jane felt heat rush through her. Millie was right. He was a handsome devil.

And she wished he'd leave so she could hurry to her truck and get out of town before he saw her. Not that he'd want to talk to her, she was sure, after their confrontation of the week before.

She hadn't seen him since then, but she'd heard plenty about him. It seemed as though everyone in town was talking about him, though certainly not in the same terms—and swear words—they'd used when talking about his father.

So far, Garrett had made arrangements to list his ranch for sale, contingent on the buyer keeping it intact, not breaking it up into the mini-ranchettes that had brought in so many people from over-crowded California during the past few years. This had earned him the gratitude of the locals. He'd also talked to the city council about donating money to build a new community swimming pool and dedicating it in his father's name. Mary Jane found this highly ironic. Gus hadn't liked kids, the ones who would be the main users of a swimming pool, not even his own. She couldn't quite figure out what Garrett's motivation was, but no one else was questioning it. They were glad to have him, and his money, back in Tarrant.

Mary Jane dawdled by the door until she began receiving odd looks from people, then she took a deep breath and stepped briskly toward her truck, knowing there was no way she could avoid seeing Garrett, or speaking to him. In Tarrant, *everyone* spoke to *everyone*.

She was once again wearing Hal's old barn jacket, jeans, boots and with her hair hidden beneath a baseball cap because she hadn't taken the time to fix it that morning. She'd whisked a brush through it and dashed out the door to run errands. She didn't have on even a speck of makeup and wished she didn't care, darn it!

"Good morning, Mary Jane," Garrett said, breaking off his conversation with Don. The smile he turned on her was mocking, as was the way he lifted his hat to her.

"Good morning, Garrett. Don," she answered breezily, not even pausing as she rushed by.

Garrett said good-bye to his friend and strode beside her. "Let me carry those bags for you, Mary Jane."

"Not necessary. They're not too heavy for me. After all, I spend my time tossing around hay bales."

"I remember," he said, taking the bags from her hands anyway. "And I'll bet you've got the muscles to prove it."

"Yes, I do," she answered, feeling those muscles go tight. "Want a demonstration?"

He shook his head. "No thanks, though it's not your muscles that scare me." He swung the groceries into the lock box in the back of the truck and turned with a sketchy wave as he walked away. "It's your mouth."

Instantly furious, her lips pinched together. She wished she had some clever retort ready, but she could only fume. Why was he trying to make her look like the villain? After all, she was only trying to protect her family. He didn't know that, of course, and she wouldn't tell him.

She had to learn to avoid him, though she didn't know quite how to do that since he was making himself so welcome in town. The selling of his ranch and the building of the pool would take time and he obviously planned to stick around until everything was settled.

Mary Jane climbed into her truck and started the motor. Didn't the man have a business manager? Couldn't somebody else do this for him?

With a sound of disgust, she guided her old truck onto the street and headed it toward home.

She wanted her life back, the way it had been in early September before she'd made that fateful phone call. Ironically, dealing with Gus had been easier than this because she'd known what to expect from him—the worst.

She didn't know how to deal with Garrett, and she didn't want to learn, she assured herself. The last thing she desired was to have to worry every day that Shannon would meet him in town, that they would see the resemblance they shared and start asking questions.

She wanted him to go away, leave her and her family alone, leave her secure in the knowledge that the decision she'd made so long ago had been the right one.

# CHAPTER FIVE

"WHY DON'T YOU take the day off and come with me?" Brittnie bustled through the door of the ranch house and helped herself to a cup of coffee.

Mary Jane started at the interruption to her troubled thoughts. She'd been standing by the kitchen window, staring out, thinking about seeing Garrett in town that morning. She hadn't even heard Brittnie arrive, and hadn't listened to the first thing she'd said. Mary Jane pushed her hair out of her eyes and blinked at her daughter.

"What, honey? Go where?"

"Over to the Blackhawk ranch." Brittnie rummaged in the refrigerator and swooped up a carton of milk. She poured a generous amount into her cup, set the carton back inside, slapped the refrigerator door shut with a swing of her hip, and turned to grin at her mother

"Mr. Blackhawk called me and asked me to come examine some papers he's found. They're deeds and land grants nearly a century old," she said excitedly. "I can't wait to see them, but I stopped off to ask if you wanted to come with me, visit with Ruth, take a couple of hours off work."

"Oh, I don't know, Brittnie," Mary Jane answered in automatic denial. She ran her hands down her thighs, trying to dry their sudden clamminess. "I've got lots to do around here." Her hired man had finally returned and she'd promptly fired him. She was back to working alone.

"I knew you'd say that," Brittnie answered, rolling her eyes. She launched into persuasive arguments that her mother only half heard.

So he'd called Brittnie after all. Had he done it out of spite, anger, what? Or was it simply to prove that he intended to ignore Mary Jane's hysteria? Had he called her this morning after seeing Mary Jane in town? When her daughter stopped for breath, she wedged the question in and had it confirmed. He'd seen Mary Jane in town and immediately called Brittnie. Why? To prove that he could?

Unconsciously, she smoothed her fingers over the scrape on her thumb. She couldn't forget the tender way he'd touched it the day she'd injured it, the conversation they'd had, the panic that had gripped her at the idea of him being around her family. He'd been furious with her, but she didn't feel she owed him an explanation. Her first concern was to protect her daughter.

"Don't you agree?"

"Yes, honey, I do," Mary Jane said vaguely, turning to Brittnie.

Relief flooded Brittnie's eyes. "Good. Let's go."

Startled, Mary Jane focused on her daughter and wondered what she'd agreed to. "Go?"

"Honestly, Mom, your head's in the clouds today. I said this is an opportunity too good to miss to see all this stuff Mr. Blackhawk has of his father's, and Ruth said she could use your help deciding where to donate some of the household items. Mom, she's working so hard over there, you can't let her down."

Of course she couldn't. Ruth was overwhelmed

with that household full of fifty years' worth of stuff. She could use some help. Besides, if one of her daughters was going to spend any time around curious, incisive Garrett Blackhawk, Mary Jane was going to be there, too.

She glanced up. ''I'll get my coat,'' she said.

''Your coat?'' Brittnie asked, appalled. ''You mean you're not going to change?''

Mary Jane glanced down at the same jeans and shirt she'd worn to town that morning. ''Honey, this is the kind of thing I wear all the time.''

''Not to visit a neighbor.''

That was true, Mary Jane thought, disgruntled. Why had she taught her children that a sign of respect for people was to make sure they looked nice when visiting them? Why did they remember everything she'd taught them, she fussed illogically. She didn't want to change, to let Garrett think she'd done it for him. On the other hand, she didn't want Brittnie to think her behavior was anything other than normal. That might cause her to think she was disturbed by Garrett, which certainly wasn't true. She didn't want any member of her family to spend more time than necessary thinking about Garrett.

''You're right,'' she said, repressing a sigh. ''I'll go change.''

Garrett looked out when he heard a car stop in front of the house. He gave a snort of disgust when he saw that Brittnie Kelleher Cruz had brought her mother along—or maybe Mary Jane had tagged along, as he suspected, to keep her little girl safe from another big, bad member of the Blackhawk family.

It amused him to see that she had changed clothes since he'd seen her in town that morning. She wore black slacks and a long, pale blue sweater underneath an all-weather coat. Good. She'd ditched the old barn coat that had obviously belonged to her late husband. He didn't want to see her in that. He wanted to see her wearing the kinds of things he'd promised her long ago, silk, satin, designer clothes. Too bad she hadn't been willing to wait for them. He could easily give them to her now.

And why the hell would he want to? He asked himself furiously, wrenching his attention away from her.

He glanced instead at the tall, pretty girl with the thick, curly blond hair that was pulled back in a neat twist at the back of her head. She was dressed in practical khaki slacks, a sweater and jacket, and looked like she could take care of herself. From what he could tell, Mary Jane had raised three competent, hard-working daughters. Why did she suddenly think they couldn't take care of themselves?

Nah, it wasn't because she didn't trust them. It was because she didn't trust *him*. That knowledge stuck in his throat like a bone from the Thanksgiving turkey Ruth had served him the week before. Maybe Mary Jane had a reason to be wary of him. After all, they didn't know each other anymore. But hell, he wasn't a monster! He wished he knew what was going on in her head. After all, he was the one who had a right to be irritated with her even after all these years. She had said she loved him, would wait for him, but she'd married Hal the minute Garrett had left town.

These thoughts didn't make for a happy expression, so by the time he answered the door to Brittnie's knock, he was frowning ferociously. Brittnie started visibly when she saw him, and Mary Jane reached out automatically and put her arm in front of her daughter as if to ward him off. Hell!

He wanted to glare at her, but he forced his face into a smile that he hoped looked a little less scary. His secretary, Jill, said photographs of his frowns could be sold as a method of frightening off charging grizzly bears.

"Come in," he said, holding the door for them and taking their coats, which he hung on a rack by the door. "I've been gathering things in the dining room for you to look through, Brittnie. Go right on in." He couldn't prevent the sharp glance he gave Mary Jane as Brittnie hurried eagerly into the other room. "Looking out for the safety of your little girl?"

Her jaw thrust forward. When had she learned to do that? he wondered. There'd been a time when she was shy, frightened of her own shadow. That was one of the things he'd liked about her. It had made him feel strong and protective. It must have been an act. Like her pretense of loving him.

"I came over because I understand Ruth needs my help." She stepped around him as if he was something the dog had left on the porch steps and headed for the staircase. "Is she upstairs?"

Garrett took an instant dislike to that cool tone. "Yes, she is. In the attic, actually." He was tempted to point out that Mary Jane wasn't exactly dressed for clearing out junk that had been collecting since the 1940s, but he resisted the urge. She wouldn't appreciate personal comments. Besides, the ones he

wanted to make to her had nothing to do with cloth-
ing.

With a nod, one that would have done any queen
proud, she marched up the stairs. Garrett indulged
himself with an appreciative survey of her slim
backside. Nice. More than nice. Too bad that pack-
age was wrapped around such a prickly, defensive
puzzle. He would deal with her later. Right now, he
needed to talk to her daughter. He strolled into the
dining room.

Upstairs, Mary Jane hurried to help Ruth who was
sorting boxes of old clothes. Ruth was glad for the
help and they spent an enjoyable afternoon looking
over the items, deciding what could go to charity.

When the first box was packed, Ruth started up
from her chair to carry it downstairs.

Mary Jane jumped up immediately and scooped
the box out of her friend's hands. ''I'll do that. Be
right back.''

She delivered the carton to the growing mass by
the front door, then paused to listen for voices in
the dining room. She heard nothing and was tempted
to peek in and see if Garrett was still with Brittnie,
but even she wasn't that obsessive. Besides, Garrett
would have some remark to make about her over-
protectiveness if she did.

Back in the upstairs hall, Mary Jane's curiosity
overcame her reluctance to be in this house. The day
of the funeral had been the first time she'd ever been
here, and today she was upstairs. She peeked into
the rooms as she passed. It was easy to see that Ruth
had made attempts to keep the house clean. The

bathrooms sparkled, and the oak floor in the hallway shone.

Most of the rooms were overcrowded with dusty furniture, which made her wonder if Gus had forbidden his housekeeper to clean them.

One room didn't share the condition of the others. Mary Jane paused in the doorway. Though she'd never seen one before, a quick glance told her it was a sitting room. It looked like something straight out of an old 1950s Barbara Stanwyck movie, she thought, looking around.

Lovely chintz curtains hung at the windows. She was surprised to see that they were unfaded, as if the shades had always been pulled securely behind them to keep them new. There was a Persian rug on the floor patterned in rich shades of blue and green as if it had been laid down only yesterday.

There were two club chairs and a chaise lounge upholstered in dark blue velvet which formed a conversation grouping in one corner. A delicate lady's desk sat beneath the window. The room was beautiful, restful and so out of character for Gus Blackhawk that she could only stare.

"This was my mother's room," Garrett said from behind her.

Mary Jane started. She'd been so absorbed, she hadn't even heard him approach. "Oh," she said, then cleared her throat. "I see. It's been kept this way for…?"

"Over forty years." Garrett walked into the room and glanced around, his face pensive, his blue eyes dark and brooding. "Dad never let me come in here when I was a kid. Afraid I'd mess something up."

One corner of his mouth crooked. "I used to sneak in when he was gone."

Mary Jane folded her hands at her waist and followed him into the room. She couldn't quite look at him because she had a sudden mental image of a confused little boy, missing his dead mother, wanting to be close to her by sitting at her desk, touching her things, and being driven out by his stern father. The image hurt, and filled her throat with sorrow.

"It's lovely," she said, because that's all she could manage for a moment. "Do...do you remember very much about her? I never knew her because I didn't move to Tarrant until I was sixteen."

Garrett raised an eyebrow at her. "I know how old you were when you moved to Tarrant," he said dryly, and then became reflective as he added, "I remember that she never lost her temper with me, never yelled."

"Must have gotten enough of that from your father," Mary Jane murmured, then gave him a stricken look. "Oh, I'm sorry. I shouldn't have said..."

"He wasn't like that when she was alive. He was happy."

Mary Jane gaped at him and he shrugged. "It's true. He changed after she died, lost interest in everything for a while. I can remember him sitting at her desk staring out the window. I used to stand by the door and watch him. Then one day, he stood up and walked out, said nothing in the room was to be touched or moved, but the shades always had to be pulled and Ruth was to clean it every week. I never saw him come in here again, but I think he must have. Sometimes, I'd find her things moved on the desk," he said, pointing to a desk set and a stack of yellowed stationery.

"That's...too bad." Unexpectedly, tears spurted into Mary Jane's eyes. She looked away and brushed at them with a surreptitious hand. Who would have expected her to have ever felt a moment of sympathy for old Gus Blackhawk?

"I guess I can understand," she admitted slowly. "My dad always drank, but it got worse when my mom died of pneumonia right before we moved here." That had been another thing they'd had in common; their motherlessness. Mary Jane had often wondered whether if her mother had lived, things would have been different. Would Connie Sills have warned her daughter away from Garrett, kept Bryce Sills from drinking himself to death a few years later? Perhaps, but Mary Jane had learned not to dwell on it.

"That's a shame, too," Garrett said, breaking into her thoughts. "That must have been hard for you." He paused. "I suppose I must have grieved for my mother the way all little boys do," Garrett continued slowly, almost matter-of-factly. "But I was grown before I understood the form his grief took."

"You mean his withdrawal, his...?"

"Crabbiness? Controlling nature? Yes. Now I think he must have figured if he controlled everyone and everything around him, he wouldn't lose what he loved."

"You."

Garrett shrugged. "I guess in his own way, he loved me."

"But he lost you anyway. Drove you away."

"Yes, and I always wondered if he grieved over that."

Garrett must have, knowing that he couldn't go back, could never be the perfect son Gus wanted.

Had he grieved when he'd left her behind in Tarrant and gone off to the army? Mary Jane knew it was selfish, but she wanted to know the answer to that more than anything. Strange, how she'd thought she'd accepted the situation years ago, but since seeing him again, all the answers she'd needed then were urgent once more.

She studied him, her gray eyes full of compassion and questions. It was on the tip of her tongue to ask him why he'd never answered her letters, had written one of his own saying she had no place in his life. She shouldn't ask. It would bring up all kinds of questions he might want answered as well.

"It seems that we understand things better as we get older," she said.

"Maybe, and maybe there are some things we never understand. I've always wondered why you married Hal so quickly after I left for the army."

She held up her hands. "I really don't want to discuss that, Garrett. It was a long time ago. A lifetime ago, and it doesn't matter now."

"Oh, I think it does," he replied, his deep-blue eyes fixed on her. "I think it explains why you're so nervous around me now. Feeling guilty?"

"Certainly not," she scoffed. "I have nothing to feel guilty about."

"Regrets then," he went on relentlessly.

"None of those, either. And I'm not going to discuss this any further."

"You *haven't* discussed it," he said sardonically.

"You've done nothing but duck the question. You're going to get a cramp in your neck from all the ducking and weaving you've been doing."

He acted as if their past was *her* fault. Her lips pinched together in a tight line and her hands curled into fists at her sides. She was so annoyed, she couldn't seem to form a rebuttal. Before she could speak, he went on, "Amazing, isn't it how your life can go from the way you want it to the way you don't want it in no time at all."

"What do you mean?"

"I mean, in my youthful naiveté, I expected us to get married." He lifted his hands out from his sides and took a turn around the room. "Live here, or on the Crescent Ranch, which my dad had bought for me."

So why had he changed his mind? Why had he written her that letter? She wanted to know, but she held back from asking in spite of the way he seemed to be blaming her. She didn't want to let anything slip regarding Shannon.

"Isn't it ironic that your daughter lives on the Crescent now?"

*More than you know,* Mary Jane thought, her heart doing a slow, sickening roll in her throat. "I…I don't spend any time at all thinking about the ironies of your life," she pointed out, proud of her cool tone. "And it's pointless to bring it up now."

"Oh, I don't know." His head tilted to the side as he considered her. "I think it's interesting to share memories, remember the way things were. Do you remember the dates we went on?"

"No."

"Liar," he snorted. "You remember as well as I

do.'' His voice went low, his eyes narrowed. ''Do you remember the rides we used to take in my truck? The moonlight picnics we had?''

''Absolutely not,'' she lied. They had been the kinds of evenings a young girl dreamed of—romantic and forbidden.

''Do you remember the blanket we spread on the ground? Making love under the stars?''

''No!'' Heat washed through her. She *did* remember that, and the baby that their reckless lovemaking had conceived. Her hands trembled and she fisted them even tighter. ''What I remember was that you wouldn't take me out in public. We never did the things dating couples do—going to a movie, to Jerry's Diner for a soda, to the senior prom....'' She cut her words off because they were sounding bitter. The senior prom was what had hurt the most. She was sure he was going to ask her, but he hadn't. The only good thing was that he hadn't asked anyone else, either.

Garrett's face went stiff. ''I was a fool,'' he said. ''We both were.''

''So why bring it up now? Let the past stay buried.'' Hurt by the memories and annoyed with him, she moved out of the room and into the hallway. ''Ruth needs my help in the attic,'' she said.

Garrett followed her out. He flicked his thumb toward the staircase. The gesture was casual, but she could see angry questions seething in his eyes. ''Ruth passed by five minutes ago on her way down to fix us a snack. You'll stay, of course.''

Her refusal was automatic. ''Oh, I don't think so. I've got chores to do, and...''

''Brittnie said the two of you would stay.''

Even when she knew she'd been backed into a corner, Mary Jane had to admire the slick way he'd done it. Still, she wanted the last word. "My daughter doesn't speak for me," she said. She wanted to get *out* of here and keep all members of her family away, as well.

"She ought to," Garrett said as he waved her toward the stairs. "She makes more sense than you do."

So much for having the last word. She knew it was childish, but she smirked at him and headed in the direction he indicated.

Downstairs, Brittnie called her into the dining room. "Look at this stuff, Mom." Excitedly, she showed off boxes of dusty papers that would have thrilled no one but a fellow archivist, along with diaries, ledgers, and ancient magazines. Mary Jane admired it all, hoping that this was the sum total of Garrett's old treasure trove and Brittnie would have no further contact with him.

She doubted that was the case since she'd seen the items that were stuffed into the attic. She might as well reconcile herself to having Garrett around for a long time. The idea made her feel edgy and on her guard, blasting away her hope of keeping her family from him.

Ruth called them into the kitchen where she'd laid out small sandwiches and a tureen of soup. Mary Jane wasn't hungry. In fact, she wasn't sure she could force a bite past the lump in her throat, but she didn't want to hurt her friend's feelings. So she took a plate, a small bowl of soup, and a cup of coffee, sat at the table beside her daughter, and listened to Ruth talk about her plans for retirement.

She hadn't wanted to quit working, but Garrett was providing her with a generous pension. She'd decided to move near her daughter in California and talked excitedly about spending more time with her grandchildren.

All the while she listened to Ruth, Mary Jane was conscious of the conversation going on between Brittnie and Garrett, who sat at the end of the table. When she heard Shannon's name mentioned, she broke off what she was saying to Ruth and turned abruptly to Brittnie.

"Shannon would know exactly what to do. She just took over the natural resources office," Brittnie was saying proudly. "And she's been wanting to get the Blackhawk ranch rangeland back into shape for years."

Mary Jane's coffee cup clattered against the saucer. "Oh, I'm sure Garrett's not interested in that," she said hastily. "After all, he'll be selling the place and the new owners will want to take care of that kind of thing themselves."

Brittnie turned and stared at her, wide-eyed. No doubt she was thinking that her mother had lost her mind; Mary Jane was one of the area's strongest proponents of rangeland management. Mary Jane gave her a mother-knows-best kind of smile and picked up her coffee cup for an untasted sip.

Garrett's navy-blue eyes glittered as he said, "I'll get a better price for the place if the necessary steps have already been taken to get the rangeland back into shape. A true cattleman wouldn't want it in the shape it's in. The only ones who'd be interested would be developers ready to break it up into five-acre parcels." His jaw hardened. "And that will happen over my dead body."

Brittnie laughed suddenly. "You sound exactly like Shannon." Her eyes were mischievous as she added, "In fact, you looked like her just now when you said that."

Mary Jane jerked, her coffee cup slipped from her hand, landing on the table with a crash and splashing the hot brew across her plate and her hand. "Ouch!" she gasped.

Everyone else was on their feet instantly.

"Mom, are you okay?" Brittnie asked, then whirled away toward the refrigerator. "I'll get some ice."

"I've got some burn ointment." Ruth rushed for the medicine chest over the sink on the back porch.

On her way, she grabbed a towel, turned and tossed it to Garrett, who plucked it from the air, one-handed. Quickly, he held Mary Jane's hand and dabbed at the coffee while his gaze searched her face. "What the hell's the matter with you?" he muttered. "Do you think that because I took advantage of you when you were young means I'll do the same thing to one of your daughters?"

A denial shot to her lips, but she bit it back. After all, if she denied it, she'd have to explain her real reasons.

"I don't know what your problem is," he said, his voice low and scathing. "But you've turned into a sick, bitter woman."

Brittnie rushed back with ice, which Mary Jane held against the burn. "It...it's all right," she said, manufacturing a wobbly smile for her daughter's sake. "You know me, I do this kind of thing all the time."

Relieved, Brittnie smiled. "Yes, Dad always used to say that if there was an accident waiting to happen, it would happen to you."

"He was right."

Ruth hurried in with the burn ointment. While her daughter and her friend fussed over her, Mary Jane looked up to meet Garrett's eyes. His opinion of her was obvious in his condemning expression. She didn't care, because if he considered her to be crazy or obsessed, he would stay away from her, and maybe from her family.

And that's what she wanted. That's exactly what she wanted. Never mind that she was sickened at the idea of having him think that of her. It was best.

"Did Mary Jane seem a little...nervous to you?" Ruth asked as she and Garrett stood on the porch and watched their neighbors drive away. She lifted the apron she'd put on while preparing their snack and rolled it up to cover her arms against the early afternoon chill.

"Yes," Garrett answered. He crossed his own arms over his chest and stared after the disappearing car. Actually, *panicked* was the word he would have used. "Has she been...worried about something?" Or was it only *him* that made her nervous?

"No more than most of the ranchers around here. She's been working like a slave since Hal died. She's determined to hang onto that place." Ruth clucked her tongue. "Truly, none of her kids want it. Becca and her husband have their own business. He's a mining engineer working on sealing off dangerous mines throughout the west. Shannon and her husband own the Crescent and are talking about turning it into a dude ranch. Brittnie works mostly in Durango and her husband owns a property management firm. Maybe one of Mary Jane's kids will be interested in having the ranch someday, but I doubt it, and it's too early to tell whether or not the grandkids would want it.''

It still stunned him to think of Mary Jane being a grandmother. And it seemed wrong that having raised her family and lost her husband, she couldn't relax, but continued working so hard.

Garrett held the door for Ruth as they both went back inside. Ruth returned to her work, and he wandered in to look at the piles of items Brittnie had set aside. He smiled, thinking he'd never seen anyone get so excited about musty old papers. She was quite a girl.

As her mother had been.

Each time he met Mary Jane, he had to readjust his thinking about her. She wasn't the warm, susceptible girl he'd known years ago. Not that he should have expected her to be, but that's the way he'd thought of her over the years.

Garrett remembered what she'd said to him regarding their time together and winced at the truth in it. She obviously thought he'd been ashamed of her, but that wasn't it at all. He'd pitied the life she'd led with her alcoholic father, and had wanted to save her from it. He'd kept their love hidden not because he was ashamed of her, or his love for her, but because he was afraid of what his father might do to her and to her family if Gus had suspected how serious he was about her.

It was in the past. Garrett knew that. It was gone and forgotten. But he kept recalling the room his father had preserved so carefully, the one with his mother's things in it, the place where he'd gone to sit and remember the wife who had died so young.

There was a place inside Garrett that was like that. A place that preserved the feelings he'd had for Mary Jane. They weren't the same as they had been. How could they be, after all these years, when both of them were so different? Still, there was a part of him that wouldn't let it go. He wanted to believe that was true of Mary Jane, also. After all, the way she'd kissed him all those weeks ago had been more than that of a lonely woman. He'd tasted desire, need, to match his own.

She wanted to avoid him, to keep her family away from him, but that wasn't going to happen. He hadn't built a successful life, a business, by backing down from a challenge. He didn't intend to start now, whether she liked it or not.

# CHAPTER SIX

*A SAD, BITTER WOMAN.*

Days later, Garrett's condemnation still rang in Mary Jane's ears. She had let him think that because she'd hoped he would be distracted from concentrating on the truth of what Brittnie had said. *In fact, you looked like her just now....*

Mary Jane didn't think she'd ever been so close to expiring from fright as she had been when Brittnie blurted those words. The worst part was that it was true. When he'd stuck out his chin and announced that the ranch would be broken up into parcels over his dead body, he'd had the same fierce expression Shannon possessed when she talked about the same subject.

No, that wasn't the worst part, Mary Jane thought as she drove along Main Street searching for a parking place. The worst part was that if he decided he needed Shannon's help, and contacted her office, there was nothing that Mary Jane could do about it. Shannon was a grown woman with a career that had little to do with Mary Jane. Her daughter would think she was insane if she told her not to speak to Garrett Blackhawk. That might have worked when she was five years old, but not now.

Mary Jane parked her truck and stepped out, her boots crunching on new snow, the first of the season. After several years of little precipitation, the people of Tarrant were thrilled to see some snow. Coming

91

early in December like this, it was even more special because it set the tone for the upcoming Christmas season.

She hitched Hal's old coat up around her neck and buried her hands deep in the pockets. Her daughters teased her about this coat, but it was warm and serviceable. She'd first begun wearing it after her husband's death because it smelled like him. It reminded her of better, happier times before he'd become sick. It had been washed so many times that it no longer held his scent, but it held happy memories. Besides, wearing it was a habit now and if she wore this old one, she wouldn't have to buy a new one for a long time. After the full weight of the Running K had fallen to her, she'd become much more circumspect about how she spent money.

Mary Jane went into the hardware store to buy some things she needed. When she saw the displays of Christmas ornaments and lights, she bought a few of those as well, and came out with her arms loaded. She didn't need more Christmas ornaments, but somehow she couldn't resist buying a few new ones each year. It made the anticipation of the holiday that much sweeter as she considered where she would put the new things. The family complained because it took her a week to get it all out and arranged. This year, she had wised up and enlisted their help. They were coming that evening to help her put up her tree and decorate the house.

She locked the things in her truck and decided to treat herself to lunch at Joe's Diner. On the way, she passed the big plate-glass windows of Lauren's Boutique and her attention was caught by a beautiful royal-blue velvet dress that hung there.

She stopped and gazed longingly at it. How long had it been since she'd had a new Christmas dress? That was an easy one to answer. Never. She'd never bought a dress to wear for a specific holiday, not even Christmas.

Mary Jane shook her head and started to walk past. If she went to any Christmas parties, she usually wore dress slacks and a nice sweater, not a velvet dress. But it was so beautiful. She stopped and turned back wistfully. It wouldn't hurt to go in and take a look at it up close. She pushed the door open and strolled in.

Lauren Wilberson looked up from the display of jewelry she was arranging in a glass case. "Mary Jane, hi. How are you?"

Mary Jane greeted her and exchanged news of their families. Lauren, one of Becca's best friends, was trying to make a go of her shop. She was recently divorced from a philandering husband and raising two children alone.

Lauren stood and came forward with a smile. "Did you come in only to say hello, or are you interested in something special?"

"The dress in the window," Mary Jane said, feeling like a giddy teenager at the idea of trying it on.

Lauren's eyes lit up. "Isn't it gorgeous? It came in this morning. I hung it up as soon as I'd steamed the wrinkles out of it. I'll get it for you." She hurried to the window, removed the dress and placed it in the fitting room, then invited Mary Jane to try it with a flourish of her hand. "It's all yours," she said.

As soon as she tried it on, Mary Jane very much feared that Lauren was right. The waist, a long

V-shape, made her own waist look tiny. The back laced together to make it even more snug, emphasizing the swell of her breasts. The long sleeves were full at the top and fitted at the wrist. The whole effect was one of slim elegance. The color seemed to enhance the blond of her hair and the blue-gray of her eyes.

"Let me see," Lauren urged. "There's no one else in the shop right now, so come on out."

As ordered, Mary Jane stepped out, feeling somehow young and absurd as she did a slow pirouette before the three-way full-length mirror near the front door.

"Oh, it's perfect," Lauren said, her eyes shining. "Even if I wasn't hoping you'd buy it, I'd still think so."

Mary Jane laughed at her friend's honesty. She had to agree. The dress was perfect. She would have given almost anything to own it—she glanced at the price tag when Lauren wasn't looking and grimaced—except pay that amount for it.

The phone rang, and as Lauren went to answer it, Mary Jane did another slow turn, adjusting the mirror so she could see the back. The best thing about it was that with all that lacing and draping, it even made her backside look slim.

Grinning, she glanced up and caught the image of a tall figure staring at her through the window. She gasped, and whirled around.

Garrett Blackhawk. Of course, it would be him. He was leaning forward, his nose almost touching the glass, his hat tilted to the back of his head as he examined her with an appreciative gleam in his eyes. He lifted his hand and formed an okay sign with his thumb and forefinger, then winked at her as he mouthed the words, "Buy it," at her.

Automatically, Mary Jane's spine stiffened and her chin came up. She didn't like being watched without her knowledge, and she liked it least of all when it was him. So why was her heart tumbling around inside her chest like those marbles of Jimmy's hitting the kitchen floor?

Garrett seemed to have changed his mind about her. If the glint in his eyes was any indication, he didn't think she was a sad and bitter woman, at least not at this moment.

She shook her head at him, indicating she had no intention of buying it. As much as she loved the dress and would have liked to help Lauren out, she couldn't afford it.

"Chicken," he responded silently.

Mary Jane made a face at him that had him laughing, and hurried back to the dressing room. She removed the dress carefully, returned it to its hanger, pulled on her own practical winter jeans, flannel shirt, and boots, then covered the whole thing with Hal's old coat and looked at herself in the mirror. To add to the effect, she jerked a stocking cap out of her pocket and pulled it on to keep her head warm when she went outside. "Might as well complete the 'lost waif' look," she muttered.

For a moment there she'd felt gorgeous, carefree, not like a woman who had a family ranch and a herd of not-very-bright cattle depending on her. She sighed. So much for her fantasy life. Time to get back to the real world.

Picking up the dress, she returned it to Lauren with her thanks, then started for the door. As she had suspected, Garrett lounged outside the shop, waiting for her, his wide shoulders propped against the aged brown brick. When she emerged, he pushed away from the side of the building and matched his steps to hers.

"Why didn't you buy that dress?" he asked.

"I don't need it."

"Every woman needs a dress like that," he said, his eyes twinkling. "However, it would have been better if it had been cut a little lower in front."

She ignored him and continued down the sidewalk, nodding and smiling to friends and acquaintances she passed. "Don't you have some work to do, Garrett? I can't imagine that a man of business like yourself has time to spend accosting women on public streets."

"Well, then you imagine wrong," he said cheerfully. "I do it every day about this time. It keeps up the image I'm trying to perfect of being a worthless layabout. How about if you let me buy you some lunch?"

She tilted her head at him. "How about if I don't?"

"Joe's Diner is right around the corner," he pointed out.

She gave him a scathing look. "I've lived in this town for thirty years. I *know* where Joe's Diner is." She didn't mention that she was already headed there.

"Oh, good," he answered irrepressibly. "Then I won't have to take you by the hand and lead you to it."

"You're not taking me by the hand and leading me anywhere," she answered sweetly. Darn it, why was she enjoying this so much? Every encounter she had with him was different, from sweetly poignant, to infuriating, to stimulating. This one would qualify in the stimulating category.

"Maybe you're right," he said. "You're not old enough yet for me to have to lead you around by the hand."

"Excuse me?" she said, rocking to a stop. "Have you forgotten you're six months older than I am?"

"Yeah, but women age faster," he pointed out, his tongue planted firmly in his cheek as he waited for her reaction.

It wasn't long in breaking over his head. Her eyes widened and her cheeks turned hot pink. "Because we have to deal with men like you," she sputtered.

"You don't even want to think how boring life would be without us," he said with mock arrogance.

"But oh, so serene," she answered.

They fell silent, standing in the middle of the sidewalk in front of the Tarrant Valley Pharmacy staring into each other's eyes. Mary Jane's breath was coming fast, her heartbeat soft and light with excitement. Garrett's dark-blue eyes turned smoky. The humor faded out to be replaced with interest and then desire. "Have lunch with me, Mary Jane," he said.

"No," she said. "I…I can't." Truthfully, she couldn't remember *why* she couldn't.

"What's the matter?" he taunted. "Doesn't the Widow Kelleher ever go out and have fun?"

The pleasure she'd been feeling drained away. Her expression cooled. "I don't see that it's any of your business."

He reached out and tugged the collar of her coat. "Why do you always wear this?" he asked. "Every time I see you, you're in this coat. Don't you have one that fits you?''

"It's warm," she shot back. "And it was Hal's."

"Is there some kind of widow's code that says you have to wear your late husband's coat everywhere you go? Do you wear it to remind you he's dead so you shouldn't be enjoying yourself by having lunch with someone else?"

Horrified, Mary Jane stared at him. That was completely cruel and unfair. Before she could form an infuriated reply, he went on. "I *know* there's no widow's code that says you have to quit living when your husband does. It's kind of pointless, don't you think? After all, my dad spent his life grieving for his spouse and never really lived again. Is that what you intend to do? You wouldn't buy that dress because it doesn't fit in with the image of the grieving widow.''

Mary Jane's eyes narrowed, her chin thrust forward, and her lips worked for a moment before she could form words. "You pompous, arrogant *jerk*. You think you know so much. You're so sure you have all the answers, but you don't have any idea what you're talking about. You don't know what it's like to nurse someone you love through a long illness then lose the fight for his life. You don't know what it's like to walk back into a house after a funeral and find his favorite coffee cup on the table by his chair, his slippers under the bed, his clothes in the closet. You don't know what it's like to go in there, close your eyes and hold his clothes up to your nose and breathe in the scent, pretending for a moment that he's still alive, that he's only in the next room and will be with you in a second if you can keep hoping hard enough...." Tears spurted into her eyes unexpectedly. "You've never lost a spouse, have you? So you—"

He'd pushed her too far. Hurt her. Garrett could see that now, and was horrified by it, but some demon forced him on. "I didn't have one to lose," he said, leaning forward until they were almost nose to nose. "I didn't have a wife because you wouldn't wait for me."

"And now we know why, don't we?" she breathed, so furious that she was barely aware of what she was saying.

Garrett stared at her for a long moment, then he drew back. "No, we don't know. It's hard for me to believe that you dumped me and married Hal because you expected that I'd grow old and be a pompous, arrogant jerk."

"Believe it," she whispered in her fury. "Because that's exactly how it happened. After all," she said, wanting to hurt him as badly as he'd hurt her. "I'd met your father. I had no reason to think you wouldn't turn out to be exactly like him."

She heard the sharp intake of Garrett's breath, but she didn't stop. Half-stumbling, she whirled away and rushed down the sidewalk to her truck, fell inside, and started the engine with shaking hands. She reversed out of the spot and into traffic without looking and heard horns honking angrily. She didn't even glance up, stepping on the gas and darting recklessly out of town.

Garrett stood and stared after her, unaware of the people who were skirting around him, and giving him curious looks. He felt as if his insides had been yanked out.

God, what had he done? Why had he pushed her like that? Said such horrible things? He lifted his hand, vaguely aware that it was shaking, and rubbed the back of it across his dry lips.

Could she be right? Was he turning into someone like Gus?

At four o'clock that afternoon, a white van turned into Mary Jane's driveway and made the trek through the dusting of snow to her front door. When she heard it, she looked out and was surprised to see that it was from Margie's Flower Shop in town.

Thinking it was the evergreen wreath her brother Dave sent her every year for Christmas, she eagerly signed for the huge box, tipped the driver then set the box on her hall table and flipped it open. It was a wreath all right, but not evergreen. It was holly, the leaves thick and glossy, and studded with plump clusters of bright red berries. Delighted, she searched for the card, pulled it out, and read, "I'm sorry. You're right. I'm a pompous, arrogant jerk." It was signed with the long-familiar, boxy GB.

Garrett. She stared, her hand went limp, and she let the card fall into the box. Her first reaction was to bundle the whole thing up and throw it in the trash, or better yet, the fireplace. It had taken her all afternoon to calm down after their encounter. She had turned to her time-honored cure of cleaning house and baking. The place was spotless, smelled fabulous, and she had pumpkin pies cooling in the kitchen, but she was still fighting the turmoil of hurt, anger and humiliation brought on by Garrett's words.

This wreath was beautiful, but it didn't cure the

hurt. The way she and Garrett had slashed at each other sickened her. She wanted to avoid him, no longer just to protect Shannon and the rest of her family, but to save herself further pain. No matter how beautiful the wreath was, she couldn't hang it. She picked up the card once again, read the message, then threw it into the fireplace where it would burn when she started a fire later. Lifting the box, she carried it through the house and onto the back porch where she set it on the washing machine. She would dispose of it later. With a wicked gleam in her eye, she wondered if the animals would like a holly and berry decoration in the barn.

At five o'clock Margie's van was back. This time it was roses, two dozen long-stemmed red ones with the most perfect buds she'd ever seen. There was no card, but she knew who they were from. Besides, he'd already apologized. There was no need for another note.

She felt herself weaken as she buried her nose in the buds and breathed in the sweet scent of fresh roses in December, something she couldn't ever recall smelling before.

The wreath was for her house. These were for her, and they made her mouth water.

She wasn't going to arrange them and set them on top of her small spinet piano no matter how beautiful they would look there. It gave her a pang to do it, but she carried the box to the back porch where they joined the wreath. She couldn't feed these to the cattle, but she wasn't going to put them out, either. There was absolutely nothing she wanted from that man.

Decisively, she shut the door and marched into

her kitchen to get ready for her family to arrive. Shannon called a few minutes later to say she and Luke couldn't make it. She had some kind of flu bug and was going straight to bed. Mary Jane expressed her sympathy and hung up. Her concern had to be set aside because first Becca and Clay arrived with the children, then Brittnie and Jared. They had Jared's grandfather, Roberto, and Hal's aunt Katrina in tow. The two of them had been dating for nearly a year and Mary Jane wouldn't be surprised if they decided to marry. They were the most senior of senior citizens, but that didn't stop them from being wild about each other.

Within minutes the house was filled with the sound of Christmas carols on the stereo, several conversations going at once, and complaints from Brittnie and Becca about the number of Christmas decorations their mother had.

"Wait 'til you've been collecting these things for thirty years," she responded.

Over the din, she heard a faint tapping and turned to the door with a puzzled frown. "I hope that's not Shannon," she said as she swung the door open. "If she's sick, she'd better stay in…bed," she finished faintly as she saw who was there.

"Garrett," she whispered.

He stood on her porch with his black Stetson in one hand and a large square box under his arm. He looked big, dark, dangerous, yet oddly uncomfortable. His boots shifted as his solemn eyes met hers in the glow of the porch light. "I came to apologize in person, in case the wreath and the roses didn't do the trick."

"Garrett, that's not necessary…."

He held up his hand. "Yes it is. It's little enough to pay you back for what I said." He stopped, shook his head and regret spasmed his face if he still couldn't believe it, then went on. "I don't know why I said those things. I..." He broke off as his gaze went past her as if he'd only now realized there were people inside. "I'm sorry. I've interrupted your party. I saw the cars, but I wanted to give you this." He brought his attention back to her, but not before she'd seen a flash of a hungry look in his eyes.

Confused, she glanced down. "What is it?" The box looked familiar, but...

"Mom," Brittnie called. "Who is it? Invite them in and let's shut the door."

"Oh, of course," she said, then hesitated, looking up at him. His regret was genuine, but so was her hurt. But of all the seasons of the year, couldn't she display the forgiving spirit of Christmas and include him? She could put her worries and fears aside for a little while, couldn't she? Besides, Shannon wasn't here. "Please come in and join us, Garrett."

He hesitated, glancing past her once again. "I don't know if that's a good idea...."

"Please," she interrupted. They'd both been such stinkers to each other, they deserved some time to make it up.

Garrett seemed to sense that, and the apology her invitation offered. He stepped forward, still carrying the box. "Thanks, I'd like that."

Once he was inside the door, the room went silent as her family turned to stare at him. She quickly made introductions, though her daughters and their husbands had met him at Gus's funeral. She introduced him to Roberto and Katrina, then seven-year-old Jimmy came up and asked, "Is that a present? Who's it for?"

"It's for Mary Jane," Garrett said, finally handing her the box, then removing his hat and coat and hanging them on the rack by the door.

Mary Jane held the box awkwardly, with one hand on top and one on the bottom. It was for her? She had the uneasy feeling this wasn't flowers.

"It's not wrapped," Jimmy pointed out. "You're supposed to wrap a present."

"Jimmy," Becca protested, hurrying up to him. "Don't be rude."

Jimmy rolled his eyes. "Well what kinda guy brings a present and doesn't wrap it? You made me wrap mine."

"You're right, young man," Garrett said, looking down at the disgruntled boy. "I didn't have time to wrap it, and I'm not much good at that kind of stuff anyway. Besides, I wanted her to wear it tonight."

"Wear…?" Mary Jane's eyes widened. "Oh, Garrett, you didn't."

"Open it and find out." He put his hands in his back pockets and rocked back on his heels as he watched her. "Please," he added. She saw a smile flickering on his lips.

Except for her baby granddaughter, Christina, who was busy trying to stuff a plastic Santa Claus toy into her mouth, every eye was on Mary Jane. With an embarrassed laugh, she set the box down on a chair, removed the lid, and brushed back the folds of silver tissue paper. As she'd suspected, it was the royal-blue velvet dress. When she held it up, the females in the room oohed and aahed over it and the men gave Garrett speculative looks.

"Oh, Garrett, you shouldn't have done this, really. It's too much, and..." And it was totally inappropriate for him to have given it to her. They both knew it. Her family knew it, and they were probably thinking up all kinds of scenarios to explain the dress.

"I owe you one, remember?" he said, his voice a deep rumble in the room that had gone silent as the breathless occupants watched the drama being played out before them.

"Why would you owe me a dress?"

His eyes twinkled. "Because of that one I ripped off you in high school."

A collective gasp streaked around the room. Becca shot to her feet and swooped her daughter up from where she'd been sitting on the floor. "Brittnie, Aunt Kat, why don't we go see if we can, uh, do things in the kitchen?"

"Are you crazy?" Kat asked, irrepressibly. "This is way too interesting."

Becca and Brittnie each grabbed an arm and hustled her out. As they went, Becca called back, "Clay, Jared, Roberto, why don't you go out and get the Christmas tree? It's sitting in a tub of water out back."

"All three of us need to go?" Clay asked. His puzzled gaze shifted from his wife's determined face, to Mary Jane's red one. A grin flickered on his lips.

"Yes, and take Jimmy with you." The women disappeared into the kitchen. The men headed out right behind them. In a matter of seconds, the room had been cleared.

Mary Jane looked at him and gulped, "Do you also yell 'fire' in a crowded theater?"

Garrett's grin was unapologetic. "Now, I didn't do that on purpose. I was telling the truth. I ripped that dress of yours and never replaced it, remember?"

"I remember," she said quietly, looking down at the beautiful velvet and running her hands over it.

It had been at a basketball game in their senior year. Garrett had pulled a muscle in his shoulder so he wasn't playing, but he'd been there, climbing up the bleachers with his friends, laughing and shoving and being obnoxious the way all seventeen-year-olds are when they're trying to impress a group of girls. Garrett had stepped on the hem of her skirt, at the moment she had shifted to avoid him. It had ripped in a huge, jagged tear.

Humiliated, she had rushed to the restroom to try to repair the damage, but it had been hopeless. She'd gone home, holding her skirt together, tears in her eyes because she'd had a terrible crush on him since she'd come to Tarrant and he'd never given her the slightest attention.

"I found you the next day and offered to pay for the dress, but you wouldn't let me. And then I asked you out," he added.

She didn't need that softly spoken reminder. She recalled that, as well. They had gone for a ride in his truck and a long talk. He had already reminded her of that. She wasn't going to think about that right now. It was long in the past, and didn't matter. She had this beautiful blue dress to think about.

"Thank you," she said, looking up with shining eyes. "I'll go put it on." With a helpless laugh, she indicated the room. "Make yourself at home. We were about to start decorating the tree. How are you at untangling lights?"

He grinned. "I've never done it. If mine get tangled, I send the housekeeper out to buy more."

"Well, you're about to learn a new skill, buddy. They're in the box marked 'lights.'" Turning, she hurried down the hall to her bedroom, listening to the sound of his soft laughter as she went.

She shouldn't accept this dress. She knew that, but she couldn't resist it. It was as beautiful as she remembered from that morning. She took a few minutes to admire it, then rummaged in her closet until she found a pair of black heels to wear with it. Not satisfied with that, she styled her hair, freshened her makeup, and found her pearl stud earrings.

She took a deep breath, told herself she was too old for such foolishness, and returned to the living room.

Katrina had returned with pumpkin pie, whipped cream, plates, and forks. The men had brought in the tree. They all turned as one to view her new dress. She hated being the center of attention, but she accepted their compliments even as her gaze met Garrett's. He smiled and it was so sweet and full of sadness, her heart ached. She wanted to go to him and put her arms around him, thank him for the dress and say how sorry she was for…well for the way things had turned out, but she didn't. Instead, she gave a smile and a curtsy that took the poignant edge off the moment.

"Hey, why were these on the back porch?" Brittnie asked, striding in with the box of roses in her arms.

"And this?" Becca asked, following with the wreath. Before Mary Jane could answer, they made her turn around so they could admire the dress. They exchanged wildly curious looks, but Mary Jane decided to answer only their spoken questions.

"Oh, I was only trying to keep them fresh until everyone arrived." Mary Jane looked at Garrett again and the twinkle in his eyes told her he knew precisely why they had been on the porch. She wrinkled her nose at him, and chuckling, he returned to straightening out the tangle of lights and wire.

Brittnie and Becca arranged the roses, then began pulling out tree ornaments.

"Ugh, Mom, this is disgusting." Brittnie held up a handful of green crumbs she'd found in the bottom of a box. "What is it?"

"For your information, it was a wreath you made me from green tempera paint and crushed wheat cereal when you were in kindergarten."

"And you've kept it all these years?"

"You made it for me." When Brittnie rolled her eyes, Mary Jane said, "Never mind, dear, you'll understand someday when you have kids."

"That will be a while yet," Brittnie murmured, grinning at her husband. They were enjoying being newlyweds and weren't ready to start a family yet. Across the room, Jared's grandfather sighed theatrically. He was anxious for some great-grandchildren to spoil.

Mary Jane chuckled, then felt Garrett's attention on her. He was watching her with a speculative look that was tinged with sadness. Guilt pricked her conscience. He had no children, saw no grandchildren in his future. In fact, she wondered how many times he'd been part of a noisy gathering like this. Not often, unless he had friends in Albuquerque who included him in their family activities.

She ran her hands over the softness of her new dress and gave him a shaky smile. She didn't want to consider that she might be cheating him out of the things she had in abundance. He could share her family tonight. That should be enough to soothe her conscience. Shouldn't it?

# CHAPTER SEVEN

"MOM, IS THERE something going on between you and Mr. Blackhawk?" Brittnie asked when the two of them were alone in the kitchen. "Because if there isn't, there should be."

Stunned, Mary Jane turned away from the refrigerator with a plate holding half of a pumpkin pie. "What?" The plate wobbled and she steadied it with both hands.

"And don't throw that at me," Brittnie admonished, cheekily pointing to the plate. "I think it would be good for you to…go out with someone, and he seems nice." She grinned. "Best of all, he's rich."

"Brittnie!" Mary Jane gaped at her daughter. It seemed she'd spent a lot of time today being speechless over one event or another. "You don't know what you're talking about." Turning, she placed the leftover pie in the refrigerator. She took a moment to straighten a few things inside, giving herself time to get her reaction under control. When had this come about? she wondered frantically. As if she didn't know. It wasn't every day that a man showed up with a new dress for her. That alone was enough to give her family ideas—which she intended to squelch right away. Straightening, she walked to the sink, grabbed the dishcloth and began wiping the countertop.

"I know more than you think," her daughter shot back. "I know he likes you. A lot."

"Don't be ridiculous," Mary Jane said, continuing her crusade to obliterate the little gold specks from the Formica.

"Mom, he bought you a *dress*," Brittnie pointed out. She walked over and stood in her mother's way so she had to stop her frantic cleaning.

"Not because of any romantic reasons, I assure you," Mary Jane answered stiffly. "Believe me, he doesn't like me as much as you think he does."

"Then why does he watch you so much?"

*He does?* Mary Jane's lips pursed. She hadn't known that. She met Brittnie's avidly interested gaze. "Because he can't believe a nice woman like me has a daughter with such a wild and wicked imagination," she answered in a dry tone.

Brittnie burst out laughing. "Wild and wicked? Because I think you should start dating a perfectly nice man? Mom, you really need to get out more and develop some kind of social life."

"I *have* a social life," Mary Jane said, tossing the cloth into the sink and glaring at her daughter. Besides, she certainly didn't know how Garrett was managing to convince everyone that he was *nice*. It wasn't a word she would have applied to him.

"Yeah, you have a social life." Brittnie threw her hands in the air. "Talking to cows."

"Don't be silly. You know I'm always busy, and I don't need you to tell me when it's time...."

The door flew open and Becca breezed in to join them, followed by Katrina. Seeing the two women facing each other, they rocked to a stop. "What's going on?" Becca asked.

Brittnie crossed her arms over her chest and moved to stand shoulder-to-shoulder with her sister. "I'm trying to convince Mom that she needs to start dating. In fact, she should start dating Mr. Blackhawk."

"And I'm telling your sister to mind her own business," Mary Jane responded sweetly.

"That's a great idea," Becca said, exchanging a look with Katrina, who nodded. She joined her great-nieces in the triple-threat lineup facing Mary Jane.

"Yes, it is," Mary Jane answered deliberately misunderstanding the point and hoping to deflect the conversation. "Brittnie doesn't need to be sticking her nose into—"

"No, no, no." Becca waved her hands dismissively. "I mean it's a great idea for you to start dating, especially Mr. Blackhawk. He's a nice guy."

There was that word again, Mary Jane stared at them in frantic despair. How had this happened?

"Listen," she said. "I don't know that *nice* is really the word to describe—"

"I saw Frank Kress in town today, and he said Garrett has offered to buy some equipment for the hospital, and to pay to have the waiting room redecorated with more comfortable furniture. For that alone, he deserves our admiration," Becca said fervently. One way or another, she'd spent a lot of time in that waiting room. "Besides, he likes you."

"That's what I told her," Brittnie said, thrilled to have an ally.

Appalled, Mary Jane stared at them. What was going on here? She'd never considered for a moment that her family members would get such notions.

Dating? Garrett? No, she couldn't. The complications didn't bear thinking about. She shook her head emphatically. "No, I couldn't do that. I'm not ready for anything like dating."

Her daughters looked at each other, then Brittnie said, "Mom, it's been four years since Dad died. In that time you've never been out with a man."

"I haven't needed to go out."

"Every woman needs to go out with a great-looking man, honey," Katrina advised.

Brittnie nodded her agreement and went on with what she'd been saying. "You've been to Denver once for a baseball game with Ben and Timmy and that was only because they're your nephews and they had free passes to a Rockies game. You've been to Albuquerque three times for your annual physicals—you've missed one by the way. You never go off to have fun. All you've done in the past four years is work on this place."

"Which is your heritage, by the way," Mary Jane shot back.

"Well, yes," Becca broke in. "But you don't have to kill yourself preserving it for us or our children. You need some breaks."

"They're right," Katrina said. "I've kept my mouth shut about this." She wagged her finger at Mary Jane. "And you know that's hard for me to do because I'm pretty opinionated, but I guarantee you no one in the Kelleher family expected you to exhaust yourself keeping this place going. Sure it's been in the family for nearly a hundred years, but no one else wants to run it. We wouldn't have minded if you'd sold out and moved into town. Hal wouldn't have wanted you to keep this place at the expense of your health, your life.''

Speechless, Mary Jane stared from one to the other of them. She knew they were concerned about her. They'd mentioned it before but never so strongly, and never in terms that said she needed to change her life, sell the ranch, begin dating.

''Well,'' she finally managed. ''I guess I've heard your opinions on the matter, but I think you could have chosen a better time to express them than at a family Christmas party.''

Turning away from them, she hurried back to the living room where the men had the tree up and the lights on. Garrett was rising from plugging in the last string. The tree blazed with multi-colored lights. Christina clapped her hands and gurgled with happiness while Jimmy danced around asking if he could be the one to put the angel on top of the tree. Clay was trying to calm him and Jared and Roberto were hanging the wreath on the front door.

Mary Jane barely heard them. Angry and disturbed, she marched across the room, grabbed a box of ornaments, and began hanging them on the tree with no thought to order or beauty.

In spite of her agitation, she had to admit that they were probably right about her lack of a social life. She hadn't wanted one for a long time and the hard, mind-numbing work on the ranch had kept her from missing Hal. But that didn't mean she wanted to start dating Garrett. Or that he would want to start taking her out. He'd invited her to lunch, but he wouldn't want to begin squiring her around the county. He certainly hadn't wanted to all those years ago. In spite of what Brittnie and Becca thought, Mary Jane knew he didn't like her much.

The other women remained in the kitchen. She knew they were in there plotting and planning. She really needed to warn Garrett about this. No doubt, he would think it was as absurd as she did.

She glanced up to find him watching her with a speculative look. She'd better talk to him about this as soon as her family left.

"Are you all right?" he asked.

"Yes." She took a breath. "Can you stay after the others leave? I need to talk to you."

"Sure," he said slowly, giving her a long look. "Sure I can."

As she had expected, Kat, Brittnie and Becca came from the kitchen to finish with the decorating. They didn't bring up the topic of dating again, but they didn't look properly chastised, either. Brittnie appeared especially devilish with her bright gaze darting from her mother to Garrett, then back again. Mary Jane wrinkled her nose at her, then went back to work on the tree.

The pleasant evening had been tainted for her, but she carried on, regaining her cheerfulness as the decorations in her home came together. She loved Christmas, loved having her family around her. Recalling what she'd been thinking earlier about Garrett not having a family Christmas, she felt ashamed of herself for begrudging him entry to her family. No matter what had gone on between them in the past, and the secret she was keeping, he now had no family at all and that was a hard thing at Christmas time.

By the time the tree was done, the children were

drooping so Becca and Clay took them home. The rest of the group followed soon afterwards. Brittnie paused in the door to give her mother a hug.

"Don't forget what I said," she whispered to Mary Jane. "Mr. Blackhawk's a nice man."

"Don't forget what *I* said," Mary Jane responded, reaching up to give Brittnie a tug on her ear. "It's none of your business, and here's another news-flash—you're not too old to spank."

Snickering, Brittnie followed her husband out the door. When they had driven off, Mary Jane took a deep breath of the crisp night air and turned around to face Garrett.

She found him picking up stray ornament boxes and placing them inside a large cardboard carton. He looked up when she came in and his smile flickered. "I don't think I've ever seen a family with so many Christmas decorations."

"It's ridiculous, isn't it?" Mary Jane looked around helplessly. "And I buy more every year. Hal used to say I..." She paused and glanced away, remembering their conversation of that morning and his accusation that she wore Hal's old coat to remind her that he was dead and she shouldn't be going out and having fun.

"What?" Garrett urged. "What did he say?"

Mary Jane reminded herself that he had already apologized. "That I was hopelessly sentimental about Christmas. He teased me about it but he didn't really care. He knew I was making up for the Christmases I'd missed as a child."

"Because of your father's drinking."

"Yes. He ruined the holiday for us every year. We never had a Christmas dinner that he didn't destroy with his drinking.'' Her head tilted up and she looked into his eyes. ''I never thought about this before, but I guess yours weren't much different than mine.''

''No, they weren't. Gus didn't drink, but he didn't much like holidays after my mother died. He growled about gifts, decorations, even a tree. It was better when Ruth came to work for us because she would stand up to him about it, but it still couldn't be called a 'joyful holiday season' like all the greeting cards wish on us.''

''I'm sorry,'' Mary Jane murmured. She had to curl her fingers into her hands to keep from laying her palm along his cheek.

''It's in the past,'' he said gruffly. ''And you'd think a man my age would be over it by now.'' He shook his head in disgust.

''I don't think you ever get over missing what could have been,'' Mary Jane said, then dropped her gaze from his. Was he thinking about what could have been between them? Maybe. She had considered it more and more herself lately. To save the moment, she lifted her hands, palm up, and gave him a lop-sided smile. ''Thus we end up with a houseful of Christmas decorations.''

Garrett nodded, but he didn't respond to her attempt at lightness.

An awkward silence stretched between them. Mary Jane didn't know quite how to bridge it. Garrett returned to his task and she kept silent, wandering over to the mantle and arranging a dried grapevine along its length. She tucked silk poinsettias into it and accented it with a few pine cones she had gathered in her front yard and spray-painted gold.

"I guess the way you decorate a house makes a difference if it belongs to you," Garrett said.

She turned around to see that he was standing behind her shoulder, examining her handiwork. He wasn't that close, but she felt crowded so she eased away from him, moving along the mantle to tweak a flower into a new position. Strange that the room hadn't felt this crowded with her whole family here. Something about his presence seemed to fill up the space. Or maybe she was absolutely too aware of him.

"What do you mean?" she asked.

"My house doesn't look like this. I hire a firm to come in and decorate the place for me. My company has its annual Christmas party there. It never looks like this. Mine's beautiful, but soulless." He said it in such a matter-of-fact way, Mary Jane felt uncomfortable. It sounded as though he simply accepted what was. If she'd heard a hint of self-pity in his tone, she wouldn't have felt such a rush of sadness for him. Her throat closed on any words she might have spoken. Instead, she gave an inadequate nod as her response.

"Why did you want me to stay, Mary Jane?" he asked. "Hoping to let me have it with a hot poker for what I said this morning?"

She smiled ruefully. "No. You already apologized for that." And she'd been thinking all day that maybe he was right. Maybe it was time for her to quit wearing Hal's old coat and living in the past. Not that she was ready to start going out with men as her daughters had suggested.

"The truth is, I wanted to warn you that my daughters think that you and I..."

His dark brows drew together. "You and I...? What?"

She rolled her eyes. "Should date," she said. "They think there's something between us."

"Oh yeah?" He grinned, but then grew thoughtful. "Do they know we used to date in high school?"

They'd done a great deal more than that, but she wasn't going to bring that up. "No."

He tilted his head. "As far as they know, their dad was your only love."

"Of course."

"I think that sounds like a great idea."

Her head drew back. "What? That we should start dating?"

"Sure." He grinned again. "Why not?"

She put her hands on her hips. "For one thing, Garrett, we don't seem to like each other much anymore, and for another, we're a little too old for the dating game."

"Now that's where you're wrong," he said, pointing a finger straight at her nose. "I like you fine. We've gotten off on the wrong foot since I came back—" he paused and considered her. "Except for that kiss after the funeral. I liked that pretty well, too,"

A ludicrous school-girl blush bathed her cheeks, but she kept her eyes steady on his. She *wasn't* going to react to that reminder even if it did send tingles of warmth through her.

"And a person's never too old to date, to look for someone to luh...spend time with," he amended.

She wondered if he'd been on the verge of saying "someone to love." For them, it was too late for that. And if she told him about Shannon at this stage, there *certainly* wouldn't be any love between them.

"Oh, I really don't think that's a good idea," she said. Apprehension formed a lump in her throat. This was a risk she certainly couldn't take. She wished it didn't sound so attractive. "Besides, you're not even going to be around that long. Once things are settled with your father's estate, you'll go back to your life in Albuquerque." That idea made her feel sick and hollow inside, which stunned her.

Good grief, what was happening to her? She'd had this all planned out so carefully, with such perfect logic. She would tell him what her daughters were thinking, he would scoff, they'd have a good laugh over it and he'd go home.

"So much the better, don't you think?" He held out his hands, palm up, the very picture of a reasonable man, but there was a devilish slant to his grin. "After I'm gone, they'll think you're pining away for me and leave you alone."

"Pining away?" Her eyes twinkled. "I may have done that when I was seventeen, but..." When interest leaped into his face, she shut her mouth and fumbled around. "But I didn't," she finished lamely. The sudden narrowing of his eyes told her she'd let too much slip. "And you don't know my family if you think they'd leave me alone about *any-thing* once they've started telling me how they think I should do it."

His face grew solemn and he leaned one elbow on the mantle. The dying fire cast an orange glow over his face. "What is this really about, MarJay?"

Her hand fluttered upward to cover her eyes momentarily. "I wish you wouldn't call me that."

"Why not?" He didn't sound surprised. His tone nudged her to be honest with him. "Because I've come back after all these years? Because it makes you unhappy? Because it makes you think of happier times? Or because it reminds you that you once wanted me as much as I did you? Or because it makes you think of when I kissed you after my father's funeral?"

Her hand fell to her side as if it had a lead weight attached. She skirted around those questions. "That was the most inappropriate thing we could have done," she protested in a faint voice.

"No, it wasn't." He stepped closer to her. "It helped both of us. In fact, I think if I kissed you now, it would help you decide that going out with me might be a fine idea."

She looked up in alarm. "No," she said. Her hand flew up to block him, but he simply folded it into his and drew her forward.

"Mary Jane, I don't know exactly what's going on between us except lots of animosity and prickliness that's getting us nowhere. You don't seem to want to deal with the past, or the future, so why don't we deal with only the present? The here and now?"

It wasn't a question that he expected her to answer. He didn't give her time. Instead, he closed his lips over hers. Mary Jane's hands came up to push him away, the heels digging into the softness of his wool flannel shirt, but then they lingered and her fingers flexed against the hard muscles of his shoulders.

Desire shuddered through her. The last kiss had only been a temptation, this one was the fulfillment. He tasted exactly as she remembered from long ago and from months ago; warm, vital, eager. He kissed her again and again, robbing her of thought, stealing away her resolve and promising something he couldn't possibly deliver. A future.

"Don't you agree, Mary Jane?" he whispered against her lips.

"About what?" she breathed.

"That we should deal only with the present? Let the past be buried and let the future take care of itself." He kissed her again, then held her away and looked at her with intensity glittering in his eyes. "Don't you think we've earned this time to do what we want? We're not a couple of kids who have to ask someone else's permission."

He was confusing her. Mary Jane blinked at him. Hadn't she meant to tell him that she wouldn't let her kids tell her what to do, to go out with him, spend time with him. She looked at his lips. Kiss him? No. She tried to focus and clear her head. Somehow it had all become confused in her mind because what he was offering was becoming more and more attractive.

"Yes," she said uncertainly. "I guess so."

A slow, satisfied smile spread over his face. His eyes gleamed with triumph. "Good. Where do you want to go? What do you want to do?"

Mary Jane gulped for air. Oh help, what had she agreed to? She needed to think, to be alone and think about what she'd done. "To bed," she told him, and earned a laugh.

"Well," he drawled. "If you're sure, but I think you're skipping a few stops along the way."

"Oh, you," she said, stepping back. "That's not what I meant."

He grinned at her. "I know, but you've always been so much fun to tease, I couldn't resist."

"Try harder," she advised.

"You're not going to back out of your promise, are you? Not so soon after making it?"

"No, no, of course not." In truth, excitement was growing inside her, filling her with delight at the idea of going out with him. "When…when do we go? And where?"

"Tomorrow night, to Durango," he said, turning away and scooping his hat and coat off the coatrack by the door. He turned back with that same devilish smile. "And wear that dress."

Laughing, she followed him onto the porch. "Okay, I will. But I'm warning, you, I love this dress and I'll wear it everywhere until you're sick of looking at it."

"I don't think that will happen." He headed for his car as he called over his shoulder to tell her the time he would pick her up. "I've got a meeting in the afternoon, but I don't think it will run late."

"A meeting?"

"With your daughter Shannon. She's coming over to tell me what would be involved in getting my rangeland into shape." With a wave, he strolled toward his car.

Stricken, Mary Jane stared after him. *Shannon.* How could she have forgotten the very reason she had been trying to keep her distance from him?

"She's sick," she called out, fighting down her panic. "That's why she wasn't here tonight."

"Oh, I see." He stopped and gave her a considering frown. "I'm sorry to hear that. I'm sure her secretary will call and reschedule."

"Or they might send someone else." To Mary Jane, that sounded like a fine idea.

"I'll wait 'til she's well," he said. "I'd rather deal with the boss." Giving her another wave, he climbed into his car and drove away.

"Of course, he would rather deal with the boss," she whispered, her shoulders slumping. "Too bad the boss happens to be the daughter I don't want him to know about."

With shaky hands, she reached up and pushed her hair out of her face, then turned and walked back into her house. She felt as if the tenuous grip she'd had on the situation had just been jerked from her hands.

Garrett drove away feeling as if he was finally making a little progress in getting close to Mary Jane. His secretary would have told him that the morning's altercation with Mary Jane was the result of his control freak tendencies being thwarted, and Jill would have been right. What was the point of being the boss if he couldn't arrange things the way he wanted them?

However, Mary Jane had defied all his attempts to control anything in this situation, showing that he clearly wasn't the boss. He still didn't know why she seemed to swing from protectiveness of her daughters, to dodging and avoiding him, to kissing him with enough heat to melt his belt buckle clear through to his backbone.

She skated around their past with grace that would have done a figure skating gold medalist proud. She wouldn't give him answers about why she'd married Hal so suddenly. He wondered if he would ever get her to discuss it.

And after the things he'd said this morning, he didn't know why she'd invited him in tonight, but he'd been grateful. He'd enjoyed the evening, being part of her family, seeing the love between them. Even the occasional conflicts and tensions had been interesting because they'd been those of a real family.

Garrett turned into the drive of his own ranch and looked ahead to the darkened house. He'd forgotten to leave the porch light on so there was no brightness to welcome him. Ruth had gone to her little house in Tarrant so there was no human to welcome him, either.

Years ago, he'd come to grips with his bachelorhood, his lack of a family life. Immersed in work, he'd seldom let it bother him, but something about the scene tonight made loneliness rush in on him.

He wanted what the Kelleher family had; people, children, conflicts, love. Each other. In fact, he wanted the Kelleher family for his own. Most of all, he wanted Mary Jane in spite of her desire to keep him at arm's length.

He'd found the chink in her armor and starting tomorrow night, he was going to press his advantage. Twenty-eight lost years couldn't be regained, but there was a future for the two of them if he could get her to accept it.

Somewhere, too, in that future were the answers he wanted from her, and he intended to get those, as well.

## CHAPTER EIGHT

THAT NIGHT began the most exhilarating and terri-
fying week of Mary Jane's recent life. Garrett called
the next day to tell her Shannon had put off their
meeting for a week and that he would pick her up
at six for the drive into Durango. Mary Jane
breathed a sigh of relief, grateful to know he wasn't
meeting with Shannon, but worried about the tightrope she was walking. She could have begged off
their date by citing concern for her daughter who
still seemed to be battling the flu. But Luke was
taking care of Shannon, and she probably didn't
need her mother fussing over her as well.

Guiltily, Mary Jane felt free to enjoy the evening.
As he'd requested, she wore the blue velvet dress
even as she still marveled at herself for having accepted it from him. She loved it, though, and she
couldn't recall ever owning anything so beautiful.
The appreciation in Garrett's eyes when he climbed
the steps echoed her thoughts.

"You look wonderful," he said. "The dress is
good, hm?" His questioning grin was so appealing
and full of charm, her heart did a soft, slow tumble
in her chest.

"It's great," she said, smiling at him. "Perfect.
Thanks again." She stepped back. "Do you want to
come in?"

He shook his head. "We have reservations at
seven, so we'd better go."

"I'll get my coat."

His swift glance told her he was thinking about the coat she usually wore. To tease him, she took it from the rack and held it out. Her eyes glinted with mischief as she asked, "Will this do?"

"Ah, well…I'm no fashion critic, but—" he fumbled as his gaze went to it, then to her face. Seeing her expression, his head tilted back and his mouth quirked. "Wise guy," he said. "Why don't you just wear your boots, too?"

Laughing, she said, "Maybe I will." She put Hal's old jacket back, picked up the black wool dress coat she kept for special occasions, and handed it to him. "Will this do?" She turned her back so he could help her on with it.

"Fine. You know, maybe I should buy you a mink, as well," he said as he slipped the garment up over her shoulders, where his hands lingered momentarily.

"Don't you dare. Then my family really will think we're having a blazing affair."

His hands tightened as he leaned closer to her and whispered in her ear. "Would that be so bad?"

She shivered at the sweep of his breath against her skin. How could he make five little words sound so inviting and yet so improper at the same time?

Awkwardly, she reached down to shove buttons through buttonholes. "Ah, well, it's a little, um, premature, don't you think?" she sputtered. Her gaze flew around the room as she stepped away from him and grabbed her small handbag. She heard him chuckling and she glanced up.

Grinning, he nodded toward the old jacket with

which she'd teased him. "Paybacks are heck, aren't they?" he asked.

"And not at all funny," she said, lifting her chin primly, but her lips twitched in an answering smile.

The stiffness broken between them, they laughed together, Mary Jane locked the house, and they headed to Durango. On the way, Garrett asked her about her family and she proudly told him about her daughters' accomplishments. When she felt she'd talked enough, she said, "I could shut up and stop bragging about them. I know I'm beginning to sound tiresome."

"I don't mind," he said, glancing at her. "I like hearing about them."

Nevertheless, it was time to change the subject. Quietly, she asked, "How about you, Garrett? How come you never married?"

The conversations they'd already had on this subject hadn't been pleasant, so she hesitated to bring it up again, but she couldn't quell her curiosity.

Garrett didn't take his eyes off the dark highway, but she saw his hands tighten on the wheel. "I know we had talked about getting married, but I was pretty messed up when I got home from Vietnam, so it was probably just as well that you'd married Hal. My dad thought I would come back here and take right up where I'd left off, being an employee of his."

"But you couldn't do that?" Even as she asked the question, she thought again of the letter he'd written her. It didn't match up with what he was telling her now.

His sideways glance was dry and self-mocking. "After spending a year hanging out of a helicopter,

providing fire for guys running for cover and trying
to dodge fire coming up from emplacements below,
working for my dad punching cows seemed a little
too tame—not that the daily fights with Gus
wouldn't have provided some entertaining fire-
works,'' he added dryly.

"I'm sorry,'' she said, and meant it. No matter
how he'd abandoned her, he'd had a rough time of
it. Maybe that was why he'd never answered her
letters. Even though he'd only been in basic training,
perhaps he'd already heard how bad things were going to be once he arrived in Vietnam, and he hadn't
wanted to drag her into that. It was a stretch, but
she could almost make herself believe it.

Still, the question about why he'd never answered
her letters quivered on her tongue, but she bit it
back. What if he asked why she'd tried to contact
him during basic training when incoming mail
wasn't allowed except for family emergencies? Then
he would ask if she'd been involved in an emer-
gency.

Better to leave the question unasked.

"It's all water under the bridge now,'' he said
with a philosophical shrug. "I moved to
Albuquerque, went to college, got a job. There
didn't seem to be time to find a wife.'' He slanted
a grin at her. "Since you got married practically out
of the cradle, you don't realize what it's like out
there in the dating game. Takes a lot of time and
attention and I was too busy to pursue it. I have to
tell you, though, it surprised the heck out of me
when I woke up on my fortieth birthday and realized
I didn't have as much to show for my life as I'd
thought I would have by then.''

The words were self-deprecating, but they struck at Mary Jane's heart. He had more than he thought he had, but she couldn't tell him that. Instead, she answered with a feeble response and changed the subject. The lives of their old school friends was a safe topic, and it carried them through the rest of the ride, and through most of the evening.

They lingered over their dinner, reminiscing about the past, but they managed to skillfully avoid any further reference to their *own* past. Mary Jane relaxed and decided that the whole evening was the most pleasant she had spent in years.

Throughout her time with him, though, Mary Jane recalled what he'd said about a family. She knew he'd missed having one, regretted his lack of children.

She had spent weeks dodging and avoiding telling him about Shannon, but she knew she had to do it. He had a right to know.

Mary Jane watched his profile as he drove her home, noting again what a strong and stable man he was. He had a right to know about his daughter, and Shannon should know about him. Whatever his reaction, she would have to deal with it. They would spend a lovely holiday season together, and then right after Christmas, when she found the proper time, she would tell the truth to him and to Shannon. It was only right, but it had to be a time of her own choosing.

Later that week, Shannon stopped by after her trip to Garrett's ranch and announced that she and Luke were giving a Christmas party. ''He's finally finished redoing the woodwork on the ground floor and he wants to show it off. You're invited, of course, and I just asked Garrett to join us, too.''

Mary Jane paused as she was taking two coffee mugs from the cupboard. ''Oh? You did?''

''I didn't get to see much of him today. After I did my assessment of the rangeland, I went back to the house, but he was on the phone with his Albuquerque office. I'll have to call back later with my report.''

Mary Jane felt a wave of relief, then chastised herself for it. She was *dating* the man, but she didn't want him around her daughter. Even though she knew she had a good reason, she felt hypocritical. A party at Shannon's house with lots of people around might actually turn out to be okay. Shannon would be so busy taking care of her guests, she wouldn't have much time for just one. Feeling like a plotting, conniving conspirator, Mary Jane only half-listened to her daughter's plans for the party as she poured coffee for both of them.

Shannon added cream to hers, took a sip, grimaced, and said, ''Does this taste funny to you? Maybe the cream is sour.''

Mary Jane drank and said, ''No. It tastes fine to me.'' She took another sip as she looked at her in concern. ''Do you feel all right? If you thought you had some kind of flu bug…''

''I'm fine today,'' Shannon said with a shrug. ''But that's happened to me several times in the past two weeks. I feel really sick in the evenings, but then I'm okay by bedtime. Then I feel great the next day until about six o'clock in the evening when it starts all over again. Not serious enough to go to the doctor, just queasy.''

Mary Jane held her cup in mid-air for a moment as she stared in surprise. Her hand went suddenly slack and her cup thumped to the tabletop. "Shannon," she said faintly. "Could you be pregnant? I had exactly those same symptoms when I was pregnant with you. Evening sickness instead of morning sickness. In fact, I was so sick at gradu…" She bit her tongue. Was she losing her mind? Spouting out that she'd been sick at her high-school graduation and hadn't known what the problem was until two weeks later when she'd worked up the courage to ask Dave to take her to a doctor in Durango? She certainly didn't want Shannon to know that.

Shannon stared and her hands trembled. "No." She shook her head. "No. We're not ready for a baby yet. I just got a promotion, the house isn't ready. We're not even used to being married yet. Besides, we've been using contraceptives.…"

"Most of which aren't foolproof," Mary Jane pointed out dryly. "Trust me, a baby's going to come when it wants to."

"I guess so," Shannon answered, staring vaguely into space. "After all, I came at a pretty fast clip after you and Dad had only been married for seven months." She grinned suddenly. "Who'd have thought my straight-laced parents would have been fooling around beforehand?" she teased.

Taken aback, Mary Jane could only sputter, "Oh, you know how it is—people get carried away."

Shannon laughed giddily. "I guess so, but like most people, I don't want to think about my parents doing something so risqué. After all, you were just eighteen."

Dismayed, Mary Jane stared at her. She certainly

didn't want Shannon to think badly of her, or of Hal, but before she could think of a response, Shannon propped her chin on her hand as she stared dreamily into space and said, "A baby," she whispered. "Wait 'til I tell Luke. He'll be speechless. He's good with babies, though," she said staunchly. "He got a crash course in them last spring when his sister Jeanette left her baby with him so she could go to Texas and get Steve after he was injured at a rodeo."

"I remember, honey," Mary Jane smiled at the ecstasy on her daughter's face. Who would have thought her math and science genius could be so misty-eyed over a baby?

"When Luke bought the Crescent, there was the sweetest cradle in one of the upstairs bedrooms. Now that he's done the woodwork in the downstairs, he can refinish it for the baby."

She drifted off into a momentary daydream, then abruptly bounded to her feet, nearly upsetting her coffee mug as she did so. "I've got to hurry home and tell him. I'll see you later, Mom."

She gave Mary Jane a joyous hug and started for the door, then turned back and with a wistful smile, said, "I wish Dad was here. Remember how crazy he was about Jimmy?"

"Yes." Mary Jane choked out the word around the lump forming in her throat. "He would have been so proud." Then before she could catch her breath, Shannon was hurrying out the door.

Dazed, Mary Jane sat, staring after Shannon. She was going to be a grandmother. Again. She had always considered Jimmy and Christina to be her grandchildren, but this time a child of her body was going to have a child. Incredible.

Not just *her* grandchild. And not Hal's, though he never would have considered the baby to be anything else but his full grandchild. Her mouth went dry. Dread tightened inside her. Garrett's grandchild, as well.

Mary Jane shoved away from the table, stood and paced a few agitated turns around the room. She had avoided thinking about this. She hadn't wanted to consider what it would be like to know she was cheating Garrett out of a family.

She stood and stared out at the sky, graying now with the snow clouds that were massing near Randall Peak. Clearly, she pictured Hal, carrying Jimmy from the barn, talking to the infant in his low, quiet way, telling his grandson some important piece of information a cattleman needed to know, and a wide-eyed Jimmy, listening as if he understood each word.

The picture changed, and she could see the two of them walking together, Hal bent over to accommodate Jimmy's short stature, and Jimmy with his tiny fist wrapped around Hal's forefinger, his chubby legs trying to keep up.

She covered her eyes to hold the memories in and to try to block out her guilty thoughts. They crept in, anyway.

Thanks to her, Garrett would have those experiences only if she carried out her plan to tell him the truth. It was only right that he know and she would tell him, but she felt the decision pushing at her as if she was being swept along in the current of a raging river.

*   *   *

"Does the mother of the hostess have to stay until the bitter end?" Garrett whispered in Mary Jane's ear.

His voice, so close, and the brush of his breath, sent shivers up her spine. He spoke to her this way frequently, leaning over as he helped her with her coat, or commanded her attention in a noisy restaurant. Now, she told herself he had to get close and whisper to her because there was so much noise at Shannon's Christmas party, he couldn't have been heard even if he'd stood six inches away and shouted. At the same time, he put his arm around her waist and drew her into a corner. These whispers and touches never ceased to make her feel hot and bothered.

Even after two weeks of seeing him almost every day or evening, she hadn't become accustomed to his touch. How could she have forgotten how often he reached out, touched, patted? He'd done it constantly when they'd been together all those years ago, and he hadn't changed. Maturity had taught her that it was a reaction to his sterile upbringing. That knowledge didn't stop her unnerving response. She always seemed to meet these touches with a jolt of sensual desire.

"Mary Jane?" he prompted. "Do you have to stay?"

"No," she said, shaking her head. "Becca and Brittnie said they'd assist in the clean-up since I helped with setting up today." She gave him a rueful smile. "I've discovered that Shannon is a real martinet when it comes to having things exactly right for a party."

He laughed. "It's rough when they seem to be trading places with you, hm?"

"Hey, she didn't get that from me," she protested. "It must be from…her father." Mary Jane's heart gave her a kick when she realized she'd almost said Shannon had gotten that perfectionist trait from Garrett. Looking away, she gulped and told herself she *had* to be more careful.

"So I can spirit you away into the night?"

The very sound of that had another battalion of shivers marching up her spine. "Yes, I think so."

"Then let's go."

He set off to find their coats in one of the upstairs bedrooms. When Shannon saw him go, she and Luke hurried over. "You're leaving? I'll bet Garrett wants you to himself. Mom, that's so romantic. And I think you're blushing."

"Don't be ridiculous. I never blush." Mary Jane fanned her cheeks comically to show that she knew she lied. Shannon giggled.

Garrett returned with their coats and helped Mary Jane into hers. They moved toward the door, and in the shuffle, Luke stood back to let Shannon pass and ended up standing between them, but a half-step back. Shannon grinned cheekily at Garrett as she said, "You be careful with my mom."

He returned her grin and responded. "Your mom can take care of herself. You be careful with that grandbaby of hers."

"Oh, now I like that—this child is nothing but Mary Jane's grandbaby," Shannon responded.

As they bantered, Mary Jane glanced over at Luke. The intent look on his face sent a chill through her. His gaze was fixed first on Garrett, then on Shannon, then swung back. His face went stiff, and his eyes raised slowly to meet Mary Jane's. In spite of her shock, she tried to keep her expression pleasant. Had he guessed? she wondered as panic beat in her throat. He knew Shannon better than almost anyone. Could he see the resemblance between them?

This was what she had dreaded and now that it had come, she wanted to push it away, to deny that it was happening. She couldn't meet Luke's questioning gaze and she busied herself buttoning her coat. After a moment, Garrett took her arm and drew her away.

The entire episode had lasted only a few seconds. Neither Garrett nor Shannon had noticed that anything was wrong, but Luke continued to stare after them with a perplexed frown on his face, his arm protectively around his wife. Seeming to catch onto his concern, Shannon glanced from his face to her mother and Garrett. She asked him a question, but Luke shook his head, planted a light kiss on her hair, and pulled her away to a group of guests.

Mary Jane walked away with Garrett but her thoughts were on Luke. Had he guessed? Even if he had, she knew he wouldn't say anything to Shannon because he would never hurt her. That was the one thing of which she was certain.

She berated herself. She'd known it was a mistake to bring Garrett to this, but there'd been no way out of it. Excluding him would have brought up questions she couldn't answer. Including him had done the same thing. Either way, she was mired in a situation of her own making. She could feel the current of that rushing river sweeping around her knees, forcing her to the moment when she had to tell the truth to everyone involved.

Garrett didn't seem to notice her distress and

Mary Jane carried on with her goodbyes even as he pulled her inexorably toward the door. She said good night to people as they swept by, noticing startled, and then knowing glances on the faces that passed in a blur. If these people even suspected what was going on in her mind, they would be dumbfounded, not just shocked.

"Are we expected at a fire?" she asked breathlessly once they had emerged into the crisp, cold outside air. She breathed the refreshing air in slow, deep drafts that helped restore her calm. If she didn't panic, she could handle this, she assured herself. *Act normally. Talk. Respond. Don't become hysterical.* Those were the things she needed to remember. The reminder seemed to help. After a moment, she began to feel better and could concentrate on what Garrett was saying.

"I just didn't want you to get started saying endless goodnights," he said, taking her arm and escorting her swiftly down the steps. "We would have been there forever."

"Oh, that is such a male response," she insisted as he hurried her along. "Hal used to say the same thing to me."

"Well, did you ever consider that he might have been right?" Garrett stuffed her gently into the car and slammed the door. Once he was behind the wheel, he didn't give her a chance to respond. "You've known people in every place we've gone in the past two weeks, and you speak to all of them at length."

"I'm just being friendly." She shook her finger at him. "And be nice to me, or I'll make you hold my purse while I'm in the ladies room."

The glow from the dashboard lights showed the horror on his face. "You wouldn't dare!"

She laughed. "Don't push me."

"Well, you've left me no alternative," Garrett growled. "I'm going to have to take you to someplace where you're not known."

"And just where would that be?"

"Albuquerque."

She half-turned toward him. "What?"

He gave her a quick glance as he pulled out of Luke and Shannon's driveway and started down the highway toward her house. "Albuquerque. My place."

They'd almost made the entire circuit of Randall Peak by the time she found her voice. "What...what would I do there?"

"Take a break," he suggested. "Your daughters tell me you haven't had a vacation in five years. It's time you had one."

"Oh, I don't know, Garrett," she said. "I don't think that would be a very good idea."

He ignored that. "I have an annual Christmas party for all of my employees at my house. It's scheduled for next weekend. I'd like you to come and be there with me."

"You mean, like a date?"

"Date. Guest. Hostess. You choose," he said. "But come and be there with me. I've already talked to Luke. He and his brother-in-law and your two nephews say they can handle your place until you get back."

"You discussed it with Luke?" Mary Jane put a hand to her head. What else had they talked about? She swallowed her fright. Nothing. They hadn't talked about anything to do with Shannon. There hadn't been time between the moment Luke seemed to see a resemblance between Garrett and Shannon and the time Garrett had headed her toward the door. She took yet another calming breath. She could deal with this, but it was happening too fast. "You shouldn't have done that."

"I had to start making arrangements. If I'd left it to you, you would have dithered until after the party was over."

Her hand came up to play with the collar of her coat. "Dithered?"

"Yes." Garrett turned into the drive that led to the Running K. "Ever since I came back, you've been alternately reluctant, resistant, and ridiculous about being with me, so I took action."

"You sure did," she answered faintly.

"So are you going to do it? Go back to Albuquerque with me next weekend and be a guest at my house?" He stopped the car before her house and turned to her.

In the shadows, the angles of his face softened. He leaned forward and took her face between his hands in a way that made her bones want to melt. Somehow, when he held her like this, she could forget everything else. The secret she was keeping, as huge as it was, seemed to shrink.

"Come with me, Mary Jane. Let me show you my home, my business. Let me show you off to my employees. They think no woman would have anything to do with me because I'm a workaholic. Help me prove them wrong." He touched his lips to hers.

Mary Jane's mouth trembled open. He took advantage of that to deepen the kiss until her breath was dammed up in her throat. She slipped her hands over the lapels of his jacket and kissed him back. If she could only maintain this moment of warmth and discovery, this island of peace in the raging storm she had created inside herself, she thought everything would be all right.

Best of all, it sounded so reasonable when he explained it. He needed her with him. In fact, it sounded wonderful. They would be away from here. The limp tightrope she was walking wouldn't be swinging so wildly over a widening chasm. No doubt, it was cowardice, but she longed to go away with him, to have peace and security for a little while before the approaching storm broke over her head.

Suddenly, there was nothing in the world she wanted more.

She pulled away and smiled into his eyes. "All right, Garrett. I'll come with you."

# CHAPTER NINE

MARY JANE wondered if Gus Blackhawk had ever paid a visit to his son's home. If he had, he wouldn't have been concerned about Garrett's success. After seeing his office building, which held the various divisions of Blackhawk Enterprises, and now his house, Mary Jane was beginning to realize that Garrett could have bought and sold his father's business interests any day of the week.

The family ranch and the other real estate holdings in Tarrant were piddling compared to what she'd seen of Garrett's endeavors.

By Friday afternoon, Mary Jane had been through a week of worry since Shannon and Luke's party. She had seen them twice. Her daughter was still head-in-the-clouds over her pregnancy, but her more practical son-in-law had been quiet and introspective at each of their meetings. He had studied Mary Jane with a faint air of disappointed puzzlement as if he was waiting for her to say something about the similarities he'd noticed between Shannon and Garrett. Luke would never bring it up himself, she was sure, because it might hurt Shannon.

Mary Jane couldn't say anything to him or Shannon, or to Garrett. She felt as if she was teetering on the brink of a decision that was going to hurt her beloved daughter, the son-in-law she liked, and Garrett, who was making a place for himself in her life and in her heart. She hoped that a few days away from home would help her decide what to do. She had already decided that this time with Garrett was important and she was going to put away her worries and enjoy it, be a gracious and accommodating house guest.

As they drove up the long, paved driveway to his home—it could more easily be called an estate—Mary Jane looked around, wide-eyed. Paddocks along the way held quarter horses; registered breeding stock, she was sure. Barns and outbuildings were neatly painted and seemed to be bustling with activity.

On this Blackhawk ranch, there was no neglect, no pieces of discarded machinery or equipment lying around, no buildings falling down.

Mary Jane turned her gaze to the house itself. And, she suspected, inside Garrett's home, there were no rooms stuffed full of old things in need of discard, no sterling silver punch bowls packed away and never used. Not that he wouldn't have had room to pack things away if he'd wanted to. The place was huge; not the Spanish style that was so popular in the area, but a variation on a Georgian theme with a wide verandah that ran the width of the first floor, roofed by a deck accessed on the second floor by arcadia doors from what she assumed were upstairs bedrooms.

"Garrett, this is beautiful," she said sitting forward to get the full view. "Stunning. The house is wonderful." She gulped for a breath and released it on a laugh as she glanced at him. "Does the doorbell play the theme from *Gone with the Wind*?"

Garrett grinned and tilted his head. "It is kind of pretentious, isn't it? I bought the place from a guy from Georgia who had visions of being a gentleman rancher. Only he lost money on that operation, so he decided to try raising race horses. Lost his shirt with that and some bad investments. Finally, he had to sell this outfit. I happened to be in the right place at the right time.''

"I think there was probably more to it than that," she responded. She couldn't imagine him ''happening'' on a business deal. No doubt, he'd gone out and found it. A company as successful as his hadn't been built by accident.

He answered with a small shrug. "Maybe."

He stopped the car, and Garrett removed their bags from the back and carried them up the steps. The double front doors were as impressive as the rest of the house, and an enormous evergreen Christmas wreath graced each of them.

"I'm sorry the wreath I sent you isn't as big as these," he said, glancing up at them. "But it was all Tarrant had to offer."

"It's a good thing, too," Mary Jane said, smiling and folding her hands across her waist. "If you'd given me one as big as these, my whole house would have tilted over frontwards."

He laughed and threw the door open to invite her into a foyer that was bigger than her living room. Mary Jane's eyes widened as she stepped inside. A curving staircase swept up to the second floor and doors opened into rooms decorated with exquisite furnishings.

"Garrett," she said. "I'm breathless. I had no idea your home was so beautiful."

He cocked an eyebrow at her. "You had visions of an old bachelor like me living in a dusty room full of books on ranch management, didn't you? Smelling up the place with pipe tobacco, leaving my dirty boots on the bed?''

"Well, not quite that bad," she hedged, her eyes laughing at him. "I know you don't smoke." He started for her and she skipped away to be brought up short by the sight of a tall, thin woman walking toward her. She had a shock of white hair and lively green eyes that went from Mary Jane to Garrett, and back again.

"Ah, Lena, there you are," Garrett said. Taking Mary Jane's arm, he introduced her. "Mary Jane Kelleher, this is my house manager, Lena Olveras."

Lena held out her hand. "It's a fancy word for housekeeper," she said with a smile as she greeted Mary Jane with a firm, quick handshake. "Your room is ready. Please let me know if there's anything more I can get for you. I'll be up in a while to unpack your things, if you'd like." She hurried away to waiting tasks and Mary Jane stared after her, struck by how much the woman's attitude and personality were like Ruth Chandliss's.

Garrett watched her face as if he knew what she was thinking. "I couldn't hire Ruth away from Dad," he admitted. "So I got the next best thing."

Mary Jane nodded, then looked around his house with a fresh view, wondering how much of the grandeur of the place was designed as a contrast to Gus's wealth and influence. She decided it didn't matter. Garrett had become a success on his own and that's what was important.

Garrett carried her bags upstairs and Mary Jane was grateful that Brittnie had insisted she borrow the matched set of luggage Jared's grandfather had given her as a wedding gift. The old duffel Mary Jane usually took along on cattle-buying or -selling trips would have been more appropriate in Garrett's bunk house than his mansion.

In the upstairs hall, he led her to a door and threw it open, then ushered her inside. "This is your room, but if it doesn't suit you, I've got four more you can choose from." He grinned and wiggled his eyebrows suggestively. "Or you can share my room. It's right next door."

Mary Jane wrinkled her nose at him to show what she thought of his suggestion, but in truth, it sounded very tantalizing.

"No, no, this is fine," she said, taking in the beautiful room. "More than fine. In fact, it's stunning." The room was a designer's showcase, decorated in shades of peach, aqua and pale yellow. The bed was a high, old-fashioned double one with a bedspread of peach-colored eyelet and masses of throw pillows. An armoire held an entertainment center and a wicker settee was placed before the arcadia doors that led to the verandah in order to take full advantage of the light. It was a room for dreaming, for relaxing. Somehow the lush textures and rich fabrics invited other kinds of dreaming. She glanced at Garrett who was watching her reaction. If she let it, this room could spring some of her erotic fantasies into full bloom.

"It's perfect," Mary Jane said, awed. Her gray eyes were wide as she looked around then met Garrett's gaze. He seemed pleased by her reaction. Setting her bags down, he said, "Your bathroom is through there, and no, we don't share one, in case you were planning to sneak in there and peek at my naked backside while I'm in the shower.''

"You should *be* so lucky!" she sputtered.

He lifted his hands and turned away. "All I'm saying is that I've seen the way you've been looking at me and I know you're dying to have your way with me, but a man's got to protect his reputation, so we've got separate bathrooms." He headed for the door before she could throw something at him but paused in the doorway. "Would you like a tour of the ranch?" He glanced outside. "A quick one? It'll be dark in a couple of hours."

"I'd love it, but I need to change clothes."

"I'll knock on your door in fifteen minutes," he said, sweeping out.

Mary Jane hurried out of the slacks and sweater she'd worn on the drive to Albuquerque, then pulled jeans and boots from her bag. She could get used to this beautiful home in no time at all.

In exactly fifteen minutes, a sharp rap on the door told her Garrett was ready. Breathless from the rush to change clothes, Mary Jane opened it with one hand while tucking in her shirt with the other. "You know, it wouldn't hurt you to be late once in a while," she said.

"Hey, it's my house. I make the rules." His gaze swept over her, approving the softly worn jeans and cozy long-sleeved plaid shirt.

"King of your castle, hm?" she asked, grabbing her jacket, her own parka this time, though it wasn't as warm or as roomy as Hal's old barn coat.

He helped her on with the jacket. "Don't you make the rules in your house?"

"Yes, and I abide by them, too, since I live alone."

Their banter meant nothing except to smooth them over a few awkward moments. Mary Jane knew there would be many more of these before she was accustomed to being in his house. They went downstairs and through the kitchen where Lena was preparing dinner, then to the barn where two horses were tied to the top rail of the corral fence.

They rode for miles as he showed her his place. She was astounded at the size of the operation, comparing it to her own small ranch. Since they were in the same business, they had a great deal to discuss and their conversation was lively.

By the time they arrived back at the house, Mary Jane was drooping with fatigue even though she'd done no real work. Added to that, she was eager, and yet apprehensive about the evening ahead. As far as she knew, they would be alone.

"I've got some business to take care of and some phone calls to make," Garrett said, nodding toward the office he'd set up in his den. "Make yourself at home. Just pick up the phone and call Lena if you need anything. Her extension number is by the phone."

"I don't think I'll need anything," Mary Jane said, suppressing a yawn. "This business of taking a vacation is exhausting."

"It's only three days," he protested mildly, stepping up to brush one of her short curls out of her face.

The warmth of his hand swept over her and spread across her skin. "I know," she said, smiling up at him. "That's why I never take vacations. A full week would wipe me out."

He raised an eyebrow at her. "I don't think that's why you don't take vacations. You work too hard," he growled.

"That's what my family tells me, so don't you start, too."

He gave her a disgruntled look and moved closer. His eyes narrowed as he studied her. "Did you ever think that maybe there are people who are concerned for your welfare?"

She lifted her chin as her independent streak surfaced. "I *know* there are, and I'm glad, but it's not necessary. I've been on my own for quite a while now and I'm doing fine."

"Are you?" he asked, his voice silky. "Aren't there some things you don't like about being on your own?"

"Such as?" she asked warily.

His hands rested on her shoulders. "Eating alone, not having someone to talk to."

"Not really. If I get lonely, I can always carry my plate out to the pasture and talk to the cattle while I eat." The weight of his hands felt good, warming her through the flannel of her shirt.

He ignored that comment as his fingers began to move, kneading lightly. His deep-blue eyes gazed into hers and she saw mischief lurking there. "In fact, there are some things that you can't do all alone."

"Oh?" She peeked up at him from beneath her lashes and was stunned to discover that she felt flirtatious. "Like what?"

"Like kiss." He pulled her closer. "Think about

it. A single person kissing the air, well that sounds pretty weird.''

"And I'm sure it looks weird, too," she said breathlessly. "I've never actually seen something like that myself. Have you?''

"No," he admitted. "I'm just speculating here. But two people, now they could do a kiss the right way.''

"Could they?'' She snuggled against him, slipped her hands around his waist, and tilted her head back.

"Yup.''

Mary Jane frowned in mock concern. "I'm not quite sure I understand what you mean, Garrett. Maybe you could show me.''

"Why don't I?'' he agreed, wrapping his arms around her and drawing her to him so that they were thigh to thigh and stomach to stomach. He lowered his head and took her mouth with his. His lips were soft and pliant, but when he deepened the kiss, they became firm. He seemed to be searching for acceptance from her and she gladly gave it. Her hands came together, clasping at the small of his back to hold him in case he got any ideas about moving away from her.

He lifted his lips from hers and stroked a kiss across her cheek. "Do you see what I mean?'' he asked.

Her heart seemed to be blocking off her air. "I...I'm not sure. Maybe you should show me again, to...to make sure I have complete understanding.''

Garrett chuckled and placed a kiss against her throat, pausing for a moment as her heartbeat drummed against his lips. "I think your understanding is pretty good and if we don't stop this, everyone on the place is going to understand a number of things.''

"Oh." She stepped out of his arms abruptly. Embarrassment blushed her cheeks a bright red as her gaze darted around. ''I forgot we were standing in the middle of the hallway. Anyone could have walked in.''

He grinned and touched the tip of his finger to her chin. ''But they didn't, so stop worrying.'' He turned away. ''I've got work to do. I'll pick you up at your room in a couple of hours. Go get some rest.''

As if she could. Mary Jane gave him a fleeting smile and hurried away. He disappeared into his office and she intended to go straight upstairs as ordered, but her attention was snagged by the Christmas decorations in the living room.

The room itself was massive, and was dominated by a twelve-foot-high white pine standing before a wall of plate-glass windows. She would have to ask Garrett to take her outside after dark to admire the sight of it all lit up with the rows and rows of tiny white lights that she could spy in the branches. The ornaments were almost all white with an occasional red or gold one for effect.

It was breathtaking, and the other Christmas decorations that had been put up by the firm he'd hired were stunning as well, technically perfect and, as he'd said, soulless.

Her conscience was pricked by the knowledge that there were no child-made decorations in his home as there were in hers. There was nothing he'd made himself or shopped for with his family.

She tried to convince herself that if a family had been that important to him, he would have married, but it didn't quite ring true. Viewing his business and his ranch had told her that he wanted only the best. Was it possible that he hadn't married because he hadn't found the relationship he'd wanted? Could he have felt betrayed by her, unwilling to take another risk of loving someone? She found that hard to believe since she'd never felt he'd loved her as much as she'd loved him. He had demonstrated that when he'd abandoned her. And yet, she was beginning to think that what she thought of as his abandonment didn't quite mesh with what she knew of him now.

The truth was that she didn't know what to think, especially with his kiss still tingling on her lips.

She rubbed her hand over her eyes in frustration and released a tired sigh.

She loved visiting here and hoped she'd made the right choice in coming to Garrett's home, but what she'd told him was true. Being out of her routine, away from home, away from the mountain of tasks that awaited her each day was exhausting. It gave her too much time to think and worry over her decisions. She had to remind herself that the choices she was making didn't affect only her, but Shannon as well, and the baby her daughter was expecting.

Turning, Mary Jane moved to the staircase and slowly ascended the curving steps, her boots silent on the lush carpeting. It had all seemed so clear in the beginning, she thought wearily.

She had wanted only to protect Shannon, but now, seeing Garrett's home and business, she feared she was cheating her daughter out of her heritage, out of knowing the man who was her birth father. Shannon's drive and ambition, her abilities in math and science were ones she'd obviously inherited from Garrett. Didn't Shannon have the right to know that? Didn't Garrett?

Years ago, when Shannon had asked why she didn't look like her sisters, why her eyes were such a dark blue, her hair black, Hal had fabricated a French great-grandmother he said had looked exactly like Shannon. It had satisfied their daughter, but whenever she'd asked about the ancestor Hal had invented, it had been a challenge to keep straight his story of the imaginary woman.

If Mary Jane told the truth now, Shannon would not only be devastated that the man who had raised her wasn't her father, but also that Hal had willingly added to the conspiracy.

*Oh, she had to stop this.* She was driving herself to distraction worrying over the situation, taking it from every angle and twisting it around like a tangle of barbed wire. Right now, she needed to rest and give her mind a break. For weeks now she'd hoped her subconscious mind would miraculously present a solution while she was sleeping, but it hadn't happened. And it wasn't going to happen. The calamity she'd made had to be faced and resolved directly. And soon.

In her room, she undressed, put on her robe, and lay down beneath the inviting, peach-colored comforter. Within moments, she was asleep.

She was here. As he pulled his sweater over his head and smoothed his shower-damp hair, Garrett couldn't help the spurt of self-satisfaction he felt in knowing that he'd finally brought Mary Jane to his home. He'd been thinking about this since he'd first seen her in September. No, that wasn't true. He'd been thinking about it since he'd heard Hal Kelleher had died four years ago. Even when he'd been experiencing lingering puzzlement and anger over her defection, he'd wanted her.

Recently, when she'd stopped being so defensive and prickly, had actually begun welcoming him into her life, he'd started to think that maybe the past didn't matter so much, after all. She didn't want to talk about it, didn't want to answer the questions that had been bugging him for so long, and maybe she never would. It was entirely possible that he could live with that. After all, there were many unanswered questions in his life. He'd never understood why his mother had had to die so young, why he'd never been good enough for his father's approval.

But hell, he was too old to dwell on those things and life was too short to let them poison the remainder of his days. He wanted to go on from here. He wanted Mary Jane in his life every day for the rest of it. He didn't know how this was going to work, but there had to be some way they could be together. Hadn't they waited long enough?

Garrett left his room and strode down the hall to hers. He would bring it up tonight, force a decision on her. He'd been patient long enough.

That decided, he knocked lightly on her door and waited, though not patiently. Now that he'd made his decision, he wanted to hear hers—not that he wouldn't try to change her mind if her decision didn't mesh with his.

When there was no answer, he knocked again and listened carefully. He heard no sound of movement. Concerned, he opened the door and peered in. His eyebrows rose in surprise when he saw that she was on the bed, the comforter pulled up to her chin. She was fast asleep.

"Mary Jane?" he called quietly. She didn't move.

Garrett slipped inside and walked to the bed. She lay on her back with her hands curled over the edge of the comforter. He reached out and lifted one hand, resting it gently in his own. Her eyes fluttered open, then closed again, but she didn't stir.

She was more exhausted than he'd thought. He cursed himself for dragging her around his ranch this afternoon, showing it off to her when she'd been more tired than she'd allowed him to see.

Forget dinner, he decided instantly. She needed to sleep. He started to tuck her hand beneath the comforter, then paused to look down at it. He'd already guessed that she was ashamed of her hands, but he saw them as something to be proud of. They were strong, competent hands, not pampered ones. She'd worked hard all her life.

It struck him suddenly that he'd never before considered what it must have been like for her, at eighteen, marrying a man several years older than she, who already owned his own ranch and had a six-year-old daughter. It had to have been a shock for her, going from a home where her father rarely worked, to one in which there seemed to be nothing *but* work.

But she had endured. In fact, she had prospered. The way her family had turned out was evidence of that. Compassion flooded through him, followed by a surge of love.

Tucking her hand beneath the covers once more, he leaned down, placed a kiss on her forehead, and whispered, ''You're not going to do this anymore, MarJay. No matter what it takes, I'm going to get you to marry me. You've earned a rest and I'm going to give it to you.''

Spoken aloud, the words were as much of a shock to him as they would have been to her if she'd been awake to hear him say them. It was the first time he'd given voice to the thought, and the first time he had seriously considered marriage since he was eighteen. It was right. He knew that. And it was long past time.

He gave her another gentle kiss, then turned and left the room.

Mary Jane woke with a start, instantly recalling where she was and that she'd intended to rest before dinner. She rolled over and squinted at the bedside clock and groaned when she saw that it was seven o'clock. Throwing back the comforter, she leaped to her feet and was several steps across the room before she realized light was seeping in through the curtains and that it was natural light. Daylight. She glanced at the clock again while her mind tried to make sense of what she was seeing.

She had slept for fourteen hours.

Impossible. She reached up to smooth back the hair that was tumbling over her forehead. Why had Garrett let her sleep so long? Where was he, anyway? She shook her head. At seven o'clock on a

Saturday morning, where else would he be but asleep?

Some house guest she was. She hurried around gathering the things she needed to shower and dress. "Invite Mary Jane Kelleher to stay and watch her sleep through the whole weekend," she muttered, hurrying into the bathroom.

*Watch her.* She flipped on the water in the shower, then removed her robe and stepped under the spray. A hazy image formed in her mind of Garrett coming into her room and speaking to her. It was embarrassing to think she hadn't been able to rouse herself enough to answer him. Truthfully, she couldn't remember what he'd said. She recalled a feeling of warmth and serenity, but that was all. She wished she could remember because she had the feeling it was important. Of course, she could ask him, but that idea made her uneasy. If she asked him, she might have to deal with something she wasn't ready for.

Avoiding unpleasantness once again, she told herself sardonically, then pushed it out of her mind and concentrated on the task at hand.

Half an hour later, she went downstairs in search of coffee. She smelled it when she reached the bottom of the steps and followed her nose to the kitchen. Garrett sat in a sunny breakfast nook reading the paper and sipping from a large mug. He didn't look up when she silently slid the door open, so she had a moment to study him.

He was wearing reading glasses she'd never seen before. They made him appear very studious as he quickly scanned the newsprint, turned the page, sipped his coffee, read some more. It was an inviting, homelike scene that sent warmth seeping through her, then some kind of emotional dam burst within her mind and she was flooded with a realization that had been growing within her for days.

She was in love with Garrett Blackhawk. This wasn't the youthful hormone-driven lust she'd known at seventeen, or the deep, abiding love that had grown within her for Hal. It was a strong surge of compulsion to be with him for the rest of their lives, to make love with him at night and wake up with him in the morning, to share her family and his work, his thoughts and hers. To share everything from vacations to vitamin pills for the next forty or fifty years.

The knowledge hit her with such impact that her knees went weak. She grasped the door and must have made a sound because he looked up suddenly and grinned. "Hello, sleepyhead—" He broke off and started to his feet. "Hey, are you okay?"

Acting on instinct, her hand shot up to hold him back and a smile materialized from somewhere. She wanted to keep him at a distance for a minute until she could recover her equilibrium. "I'm fine," she answered breezily. "I was...startled to see you up so early, thought you might be the type to sleep in on Saturdays."

His grin returned, this time spiced with a wicked slant. "Only if I've got a reason to."

She gave him a scolding look and he laughed as he headed for a cabinet and removed a mug. He poured her some coffee and offered breakfast. "You must be starved. You haven't eaten since lunch yesterday," he said.

"You shouldn't have let me sleep so long," she responded, taking the mug and adding cream.

"Well, I was afraid I'd probably bored you into a coma dragging you around the ranch yesterday, so I figured I'd better let you sleep it off."

Mary Jane smiled, and within a few moments, they seemed to be back to the easy affinity they'd had the day before. She knew something had changed within her, however. The realization that she loved him had added another layer to the weight of her concerns. All the issues she'd been avoiding were lining up like dominoes. One would fall and then the others would follow, crushing her good intentions. She had to tell him everything, and soon, but it couldn't be today. There was too much to do and she felt it was important that she talk to Shannon first.

Lena hurried in, full of plans for what needed to be accomplished that day for the upcoming party. Garrett and Mary Jane were quickly swept up into the tornado of activity.

That evening, the house filled up with Garrett's employees. They greeted her with interest, especially his secretary, Jill, who looked Mary Jane up and down exactly as she had the day before at his office. Only this time, she gave Mary Jane a hug while signaling a thumbs up to Garrett that made him laugh.

The party passed in a happy blur of dancing, singing, and exchanging of gifts. Mary Jane had a gift for Garrett, a black-and-white photo of the Blackhawk Ranch that dated from the 1940s. She'd had a new, clean print made from a stained, grainy original Brittnie had found.

When the party finally ended and the last guests had departed, it was well after midnight. Drooping with fatigue, Lena headed for her own small house behind the main one. She waved a hand at the messy rooms as she passed. "All of this can be cleaned up tomorrow," she declared. "And anyone who disturbs my sleep before noon had better have a darned good reason."

"Yes, ma'am." Garrett saluted her as she disappeared, then turned to Mary Jane. "Alone at last," he intoned, his dark eyes shining. "Come into the den with me. I have something for you." He took her hand and pulled her along with him to the small room that opened off the entryway.

Mary Jane had noticed it hadn't been open to the other guests, and when he ushered her inside, she saw why. This was Garrett's private sanctuary. His favorite books were arranged on shelves lining the walls, personal mementos and collections were displayed in glass cases. Before the fireplace there was a bottle of champagne in a bucket of ice and two glasses on a tray. A fire was laid in the fireplace. Garrett went straight to it, lit it, then turned to her and held out his hand.

"Come here, MarJay," he said, his eyes dark and compelling in the firelight.

His use of that old pet name never failed to make her feel weak. Hesitantly, she crossed to him and laid her hand in his.

"We're going to celebrate with champagne," he said, gathering her close for a kiss. He released her, opened the bottle, and poured some for each of them. He touched the rims of their glasses together.

"What are we celebrating?" she asked, dutifully

sipping from the glass. Busy with guests, she'd had very little to eat that evening. The fizzy drink went straight to her head, making the room swirl pleasantly.

"I'll show you," he said mysteriously, stepping to his desk, and removing something from a drawer. When he came back to her, he held a small box in his hand. Flipping the lid open, he held it out to her.

She found herself staring at a ring, its stone a deep, dark-blue sapphire the exact color of his eyes. It was surrounded by a circle of diamonds.

The champagne. It was causing her to hallucinate. Blinking, she gazed up at him. Through dry lips, she whispered, "Garrett, what…?"

"Marry me, MarJay," he said. "Twenty-eight years later than we should have, but marry me."

She looked at him, then at the ring. "Garrett, I…" Her hands began to tremble, sloshing the remaining champagne to the rim of her glass. He took it gently from her and set it down.

"I had a friend of mine open his jewelry store at nine o'clock last night so I could get it." Humor and pride echoed in his voice.

She barely heard him, mesmerized by the ring as dozens of questions and protests whizzed through her mind. "I…don't know what to say."

His eyes narrowed beneath his thick brows. "'Yes' would be a good start. And don't say this is so sudden. What did you think I've been leading up to?"

She licked her dry lips. The love for him she had rediscovered that morning prompted her to accept, but there were barriers, ones he didn't even suspect. "I…I didn't think…"

"Well, start thinking," he suggested harshly, snapping the lid shut on the box. Obviously disappointed by her reaction, he said, "Is it Hal? Are you still so in love with your husband you can't marry me?"

"I'll always love Hal, but I didn't bury myself with him."

"Then what is it?"

"I need time, " she said, giving him an anguished look. "There are things I need to resolve...." She wanted so badly to tell him the truth, but she knew he would be furious, and she felt compelled to speak to Shannon first. She had always been close to her daughter, and felt she would be more understanding, giving her the courage to face Garrett.

Garrett studied her for a long moment, then his face softened. "Then resolve them. But do it fast. I've waited twenty-eight years, and I'm tired of waiting." His face softened as he took her in his arms once again and kissed her. "Have mercy, Mary Jane. Hasn't it been long enough?"

Mary Jane wrapped her arms around him and tucked her head under his chin, wishing she never had to leave the haven of his arms. "All right, Garrett, I'll resolve everything," she promised.

But once things were resolved, would he want her? That was the question that crushed her.

# CHAPTER TEN

"So much for best-laid plans," Garrett muttered as he drove away from Mary Jane's house. He had left her there after they'd driven home in a strained silence. He hadn't exactly sprung it on her, he told himself. After the way he'd chased her all over the county, manufactured meetings with her, sent flowers and Christmas wreaths, showed up at her door with the dress she loved, taken her out every night for two weeks, convinced her to go home with him, he was sure she'd known what was in his mind.

Garrett punched the car's accelerator and swept onto the highway leading to his own ranch. He loved her, damn it. He'd loved her since he was seventeen. He refused to believe she didn't feel the same way, in spite of having been married to Hal for all those years. She had loved Hal. Garrett was certain of that. She wasn't the type of woman to marry a man she didn't love. It was still hard for him to accept the fact that she'd been involved with Hal and him at the same time, but that was all in the past. Hal was gone, and Garrett was here, ready to marry her.

What was holding her back? Her ranch? That was easily solved. He'd be glad to pay top wages to hire the best ranch manager in the business to run it for her. It was something more, something that had her deeply worried. Whatever it was, she'd promised to resolve it. Garrett could only hope she would do it soon.

Garrett lifted his shoulders restlessly. He wasn't used to waiting for something this important. When he'd left the army, he'd vowed that he would run his own life, never again be managed by his father, a superior officer, finances, anything. From that day, he'd managed matters exactly as he'd wanted them to be—until he'd met Mary Jane again. Since then, things didn't seem to be going the way he planned.

It annoyed him that he couldn't take over, solve the problem—whatever the hell it was—and be done with it. He couldn't do that. He'd never been married, but he had a pretty good idea that barreling in and controlling her life wouldn't be a very auspicious beginning to wedded bliss.

His mind on Mary Jane, he had driven up beside the Blackhawk ranch house and parked the Lincoln before he realized there was another car already there. He frowned, then smiled when he realized it belonged to Brittnie Cruz. She must have come back to work on the items he was giving to the historical society. He grabbed his bags and hurried into the house.

As soon as he closed the front door, Brittnie hurried from the dining room where she'd set up a laptop computer on which she was compiling her inventory.

She greeted him with a grin as he set down his bag and briefcase and folded her arms over her chest, much in the pose of an irate parent. Her eyes, so much like Mary Jane's, teased him. "Well, well, here he is, the man who spirited my mother away for the weekend. What do you have to say for yourself?"

He grinned and chucked her under the chin. He

liked her, liked all of Mary Jane's family, especially Shannon, with whom he seemed to share a special bond of good-natured understanding. He couldn't wait to make them his own.

"I say we had a fine time, your mom got some much-needed rest, and anything else you want to know will go unanswered—at least by me."

Brittnie laughed and began excitedly to tell him about the discoveries she'd made. He got a real kick out of her. He'd never met anyone who got so excited about old books and papers.

"I found something at the bottom of a box that I think you'd better open yourself," she said. She turned back to the table, and picked up a square green metal box, the kind his father had kept canceled checks in years ago. On the top, the words *Personal and Confidential* had been written in indelible marker.

Garrett's eyebrows lifted in surprise as he took the box from her. The handwriting was his father's, but he'd never seen this particular box before. A metal clasp on the front was locked. No doubt, the key was long-lost. He would have to force the lock. "Thanks, Brittnie," he said. "I'll let you know if it's anything for the collection you're compiling."

Her lively gray eyes met his. "Maybe they're your parents' love letters, Garrett. You might want to keep them." She moved away and picked up her coat. "I'm quitting for the day. Ruth is already gone, but she said to tell you she left a casserole for your dinner."

Intrigued by the box, Garrett barely nodded as she breezed out the door. He went into the kitchen and searched through drawers until he found the large screwdriver and hammer Ruth kept there. Setting the box on the table, he inserted the tip of the screwdriver into the hasp and pounded it with the hammer until it broke.

Flipping the box open, he looked inside, then went very still when he saw that the one on top was addressed to him and had a postmark that was twenty-eight years old. Slowly, he picked it up and stared at it, then glanced at the one remaining in the box.

They were letters, all right, but they weren't the love letters of his parents.

Mary Jane had finished unpacking and was standing in her kitchen opening two days' worth of mail when she heard the slam of a car door out front. She had barely made it to the kitchen doorway when footsteps pounded on the porch, and then her front door swept open.

Garrett stood there, his face red and his eyes murderous. There was a white line of fury around his mouth as he stalked into her living room.

Her hand flew to her throat. "Why, Garrett, what is it? What's wrong?"

"This." His hand shot up and she could see that he was clutching some papers.

They whipped past her face before she could even identify them, but a knot of dread formed in her stomach, then rose into her throat. "What are they?"

"Any idiot could see they're letters. Ones you wrote to me." He held them out to her.

"So?" she murmured, taking them. The thing she had been dreading and trying to avoid was breaking over her head, but she didn't fully understand his fury.

"So?" he asked incredulously. "The only thing you can say is '*So*'?"

She looked up, confused. "Garrett, it's not as if you haven't seen—"

"They're self-explanatory," he interrupted in a full-voiced roar. "Reading between the lines of those old letters has told me something I should have known a lifetime ago. Shannon's lifetime, to be exact. She's my daughter, isn't she? And you've kept her from me all these years. You let her grow up thinking another man was her father!"

"Excuse me?" she shouted back. "*Now* these letters make sense to you? When you first read them twenty-eight years ago, you couldn't see between the lines and figure that out?" She waved them in front of his nose. "I said I desperately needed to talk to you, begged you to call me, write me, come see me, *anything,* because there was something important I had to tell you."

His chin thrust out. "What the hell are you talking about? I've never seen these before."

"Don't lie to me, Garrett." She slapped the letters against her hand. "I wrote these to you and the only response I got was a letter saying it was all over between us, that you'd realized you were too young to get involved with someone…someone…" Mary Jane was furious to realize her voice was about to break. She forced the words out. "Like me!"

"I never wrote any such damned thing! And I never saw those letters before I found them in a locked box at my dad's house."

They were standing toe to toe, yelling into each

other's faces when the truth struck them simultaneously.

"My dad," Garrett said, his voice shaking. His eyes met hers, which were equally horrified. He opened and closed his mouth a couple of times, then he swallowed hard.

Dazed, he glanced at the letters she held. "I didn't think…I was so furious with you when I saw them. They were in that box, in his house because he stole them." He glanced down at the envelopes in her hand. "But they were mailed. They're postmarked…"

"*My* dad." This time it was Mary Jane who said the words as a sick feeling rolled up in her throat. "He stole them. He worked at the post office for a short time after you left for the army." She shook her head, wanting to deny it. "He said a friend had gotten him the job, maybe…maybe it was your dad, but…but after a little while, he quit and left town, said he didn't need the job anymore. I wonder if your father paid him.…" She shook her head again, still unable to comprehend what was staring her in the face. "He couldn't have stolen them. Tampering with the mail is a federal crime."

Garrett laughed harshly. "That wouldn't have stopped either of our dads. Mine must have paid yours to steal your letters, keep us apart." He focused on her intently. "You said I wrote to you. What did you mean?"

"After I mailed these, I heard back from you. Got a typed letter saying you…had nothing in common with me. You'd realized you didn't love me. I wasn't the one for you. You said you had things to do with your life that didn't include me. It was signed the way you always signed notes to me, with that crazy boxy G you used. In it, you called me MarJay,'' she whispered. She lifted a stricken face to him. ''I threw that letter away, I was so furious. I thought you'd been using me.'' She lifted her hands helplessly. ''The town drunk's daughter.''

Garrett shook his head slowly, still trying to take it in. ''He must have looked through my things and found a note I'd written and didn't give you in…one of my textbooks or something.'' He reached up and slowly ran his hand over his face. ''He didn't want me to go out with you, but I never expected him to do something like that. I never considered…'' Garrett focused on her. ''I was never ashamed of you because of your family. But even if you thought that, why didn't you try harder to contact me?''

''Oh come on, Garrett, I was eighteen years old. Scared out of my mind. I had no money, no job, no family support except for my brother who only had a minimum-wage job, a letter from you saying you wanted nothing more to do with me. Why would I have continued to contact you?''

Garrett stared at her for a second, then ran a hand through his hair. His face was grim, devastated. ''So you married Hal?''

''He was my brother David's best friend. He'd always liked me, been kind to me. He'd been happy in his marriage, and wanted to be married again, needed a mother for Becca. I didn't know what else to do. I had no money, no skills, and there he was, offering to take care of me. He was a good husband. He was there for me, taking care of things. He never showed anything except pride in me as his wife. I came to love him. And he…he never in any way thought of Shannon as being anything but his own daughter.''

"But she wasn't," Garrett said, his voice as hard as tempered steel. "She was, *is,* my daughter. And she's about to have my grandchild.''

"You won't tell her," Mary Jane insisted, lifting a shaking hand to point at him. "Don't you dare tell her you're her father.''

"Will you?''

"In time, I…''

"Now," he shouted in cold fury. "Or I'll tell her. You've kept her from me her whole life. I have a right to know my daughter and she has the right to know that I'm her father. I have no other child," he said, lifting his hand and slashing it through the air. "I want to know the one I've got.…''

"Oh, come on, Garrett, not having children was your choice, you could have married.…''

"I was in love with you. From the time I was seventeen, I never stopped loving you. I could have married someone else, but how could I know she wouldn't betray me the way you had?''

"I didn't!''

"But I didn't know that, did I, because the truth was kept from me. *You* kept it from me. You could have tried harder, let me know you were expecting my baby. Well, now you've got a choice to make," he went on relentlessly. "Either you tell Shannon the truth, or I will." He turned and stomped out, shoving the storm door open so hard it rocked on its hinges. The porch boards clattered under the force of his feet as he stalked to his car, jumped in and roared away, spurting gravel up from behind his tires.

Mary Jane dashed after him. "Garrett, no. You can't do this. Don't…" She was shouting at a rooster-tail of dust left by the tires of his car.

With a desperate moan, she collapsed on the porch steps and covered her face with her hands. The calamity she feared had happened before she was ready to deal with it. Her mind scrambled for a solution, but there was only one. She had to get to Shannon before he did. Staggering to her feet, she lurched inside. A glance at the clock told her Shannon would be home from work by now.

Moving as if she'd received a blow to the head, she found the keys to her truck, and somehow maneuvered herself into it, started the motor, and headed to the Crescent Ranch.

Worried and distracted, she barely remembered the trip, but she stopped before the big ranch house and stumbled up the stairs. She had no words to say what she had dreaded saying all of Shannon's life. She knew she had fooled herself into thinking Shannon would never know. She should have guessed that something like this would happen, that Garrett would return someday and the past she'd thought was buried and resolved would surface again. But so swiftly, angrily—she hadn't expected that.

Her knock was answered immediately by Shannon, still dressed in the long-sleeved shirt and jeans she wore for field work. Her thick black hair was pulled back in its usual french braid. She flung the door wide. "Hi, Mom, how was Albuquerque? I…" she focused on her mother's devastated face and her arms swept out. "Mom, what's the matter?"

Mary Jane clasped her daughter to her, gazed into

her face, then reached up and brushed soft black hairs from her cheek. Tears filled her eyes. What she would say in the next few minutes would alter their relationship in ways she could only guess. In terms of the old cliché, she feared the worst and hoped for the best.

"Sweetheart, I...I need to talk to you," she said in a shaky voice. "Is Luke around? I think he should be here."

Alarmed, Shannon, stammered. "Y-yes. Come sit down." She supported Mary Jane as she helped her to an overstuffed chair by the fireplace. "I'll go get him." After settling her mother, she dashed from the room, shouting Luke's name.

"No, no. It can't be true," Shannon said, her voice rising, then breaking. Frantic, she looked from Mary Jane to Luke, and back. "Garrett Blackhawk? My father? No."

Mary Jane leaned forward and clasped Shannon's fingers. Their four hands were cold, communicating a terrible chill between them. She had told the whole story to her horrified daughter who had sat in the circle of her husband's arm with a look of acute shock and disbelief on her face.

"I'm so sorry, honey," Mary Jane said. Her heart ached for her daughter, but now that the truth was out, she felt she needed to focus on reassuring her of the profound love of her parents. "Hal and I never wanted you to know. As far as he and I were concerned, and the rest of the world, too, he was your father. I had to tell you the truth now because Garrett has found out and he threatened to tell you if I didn't."

Now that she had calmed down, Mary Jane had begun to doubt that he would have carried out his threat. It didn't matter because she had finally unburdened her heart and now she could do no more than try to help Shannon deal with the truth.

Shannon pulled away from both Mary Jane and Luke and stood. "I...I feel sick...." She lurched toward the stairs. Luke strode up to her, swept her into his arms, and carried her up, murmuring softly to her as he went.

Mary Jane was left alone, feeling hollow and curiously detached as if this calamity was happening to someone else. The sensation didn't last long because the truth crashed down on her. She had devastated her beloved daughter. Soon Becca and Brittnie would have to know, and before long, everyone in Tarrant, as well. This nightmare would go on and on, bringing fresh pain with each retelling.

She sat with her head in her hands trying to summon the strength to stand up, only managing to rouse herself when she heard footsteps on the stairs. She looked up to see Luke descending.

"She's going to rest," he said. He stood before her with his cattleman's hands dangling as if each one weighed ten pounds. His face was grim and anxious for his wife.

Mary Jane scrambled to her feet. "I'll go to her..."

"No, you've done enough," he said, not unkindly. "She's got to begin coming to terms with it on her own."

"I've hurt her." Mary Jane shook her head in distress.

"But not intentionally. Deep down, she knows that, knows that everything you and Hal did was for her good. Mary Jane, you've raised a strong daughter, but you've got to give her time to remember that on her own."

Lifting her eyes to his compassionate ones, her lips trembled as she said, "You guessed, didn't you?"

He tilted his head. "I had my suspicions during the Christmas party here. She and Garrett are really very much alike."

"I know, I couldn't believe no one else seemed to see it. That *they* didn't seem to see it. If you guessed, why didn't you tell her what you suspected?"

His smile was sad. "It wasn't my secret to tell, Mary Jane, but I'll be honest and say I knew it would have to be told soon."

Nodding, Mary Jane turned away. "And now it has."

"It's going to be all right," he said, reaching out to grasp her shoulder. "It'll take time, but it will be all right. It's hit her especially hard right now because of the baby and all."

"She shouldn't be having this kind of upset," Mary Jane mourned.

"What's done is done," Luke said. "Strangely enough, she's the one who taught me that. I guess she learned that from you and Hal."

Mary Jane gave him a hug, grateful for his comforting words. She glanced around vaguely. "I'd better go home." She started for the door, but turned back with tears in her eyes. "Take care of her. And let me know how she is."

"I will," he promised as he headed back upstairs to his grieving wife.

Mary Jane let herself out into the chill night air. She realized with a slight shock that she'd been so distraught she hadn't worn a coat, not even Hal's old one, when she'd left her house. Shivering, she climbed into her truck and drove home, feeling curiously light-headed and detached.

Luke had spoken the truth. What's done was done, and she couldn't change it. She had raised a strong daughter who would eventually be able to deal with this. It might affect the closeness of their relationship, but Mary Jane didn't know that for certain yet. No point in borrowing trouble.

But what about Garrett? Mary Jane loved him. She wanted to marry him, but what he'd said was justified. Her intentions had been only the best, but the ultimate result was that she'd kept his daughter from him. She didn't know if he could forgive her for that.

Mary Jane woke at dawn from an uneasy sleep punctuated by troublesome dreams featuring her angry family members, and an even angrier Garrett. She had tried to call him when she'd returned home last night to tell him she'd spoken to Shannon. There had been no answer, so she had tortured herself with imagining that he'd gone to a bar in town, driven to Albuquerque, flown off the face of the earth, silly worries that did nothing to help her state of mind.

She dragged herself into the shower, then dressed and headed for the kitchen to make herself some breakfast, though she didn't know why she bothered.

It would have no more taste than the dinner she'd tried to choke down last night.

After breakfast, the day dragged, as did the one after that. She went to the phone a dozen times to call either Shannon or Garrett, but stopped before picking up the receiver. They both needed time to accustom themselves to the news and she knew it wouldn't help for her to force things no matter how much she wanted to reclaim the close relationship with her daughter or tell Garrett how sorry she was and how much she loved him.

Waiting was hard, though, making her sad and sick at heart. She could hardly sleep, lying awake long into the night, then falling asleep to dream unhappy scenarios in which neither Shannon nor Garrett could forgive her. She woke early on the third morning, her mind full of Shannon and Garrett, dressed, and went to make coffee.

She was waiting for the coffee to finish dripping into the pot when the sound of a car drew her to the front of the house. Her heart leapt with joy when she saw that it was Shannon's car. Squinting through the pale light, she saw that there was someone with her. Was it Luke? No, Garrett.

She threw the front door open and hurried onto the porch, clasping her arms around herself to ward off the chill.

''Shannon, Garrett,'' she said, her eyes brimming with more of the tears she'd been shedding for three nights.

Her daughter jumped from the car and dashed up the steps. Her face was pale and ravaged, but she looked more at peace than she had the last time her mother had seen her. "Mom," she answered, rushing to hug her.

Mary Jane wrapped her arms around her, kissed her cheek repeatedly, and pulled her inside, leaving the door open so Garrett could follow. "Are you okay, sweetheart?" she asked, her trembling hands running lightly over Shannon's face. "I was so worried, but I knew I needed to give you time...."

"I'm fine, Mom," Shannon assured her, then glanced over her shoulder. "I called Garrett last night. He came to the house and we talked, then he came back this morning so we could drive here together."

Mary Jane's glance flew from Shannon to Garrett. His face was solemn, watchful. "Is it...all right?"

"Yes. It's going to take me a while to sort things out, but I'll be okay." She shrugged. "This changes the way I've always thought of myself, but Hal Kelleher was my dad, and I know the decisions you and he made were what you thought were best for me."

With trembling hands, Mary Jane framed Shannon's beautiful face once again. "He would be proud to hear you say that because it's true. We never wanted you to be hurt."

With a nod, Shannon gave her mother another kiss and said, "I've got to get to work, but I'll see you later, okay?"

With another tearful hug, Mary Jane let her go, grateful for the way matters seemed to be resolving themselves.

When Shannon was gone, Mary Jane closed the front door and turned to Garrett, who stood in the middle of her living room, with his coat still on and his hat in his hand.

She could see that his eyes were rimmed with exhaustion that matched hers, but she read peace in them that she hadn't seen when he had stormed out on Monday. It had helped for him to talk to Shannon.

Licking her lips, she pressed her hands together in front of her and asked hesitantly, ''How about you, Garrett? Are you all right?''

One corner of his mouth twisted up. He tossed his hat onto the sofa, then unbuttoned his jacket and laid it aside. ''That depends on whether or not you can forgive me for acting like a jackass. I said some things…''

''You were in shock. It's understandable.''

He reached up to pinch the bridge of his nose. ''I sounded like Gus, spouting demands, laying down the law.'' Garrett's hand fell away and he gave her an agonized look. ''He must have known.''

''About Shannon, you mean?''

''Yes. He was a smart man. He would have read between the lines and known the reason you needed to see me was to tell me you were pregnant. Then, he would have seen Shannon around, with her black hair and blue eyes, and he would have known.''

''I always thought he knew,'' Mary Jane admitted. ''It's one of the reasons he's always hated us. He tried to buy Hal out to get rid of all of us, but Hal wouldn't sell. Gus was a bitter old man because he'd lost you, driven you away, tossed away his only chance to be a grandfather.''

''It ate at him,'' Garrett said. ''The last words he said to me were that he'd been right to 'run you off,' that you weren't good enough for me—sounds exactly like that letter he wrote to you and signed my name, doesn't it? To the very end he was trying to justify the terrible thing he'd done.''

"I feel sorry for him. In fact, I always did." She paused, then squared her shoulders. "You were right. If I'd tried harder I could have reached you. I took that letter at face value, too young and scared and foolish to realize that you really did love me and wouldn't have abandoned me like that, but..."

"What?" Garrett stepped closer. His hands lifted as if he wanted to hold her, then fell to his sides.

"Like I said, I convinced myself you were ashamed of me because I was the daughter of Bryce Sills, the town drunk. We never went where the other kids went. I hoped you'd take me to the senior prom, but you didn't."

Regret spasmed his face. "I was never ashamed of you. You've got to believe that. I always loved you, but I knew if I took you out where people would see us, it would get back to my dad and he'd make our lives hell. I was too young and intimidated by him to realize he was going to do that, anyway. I thought that if I did what he wanted, joined the army, made him proud of me by becoming a hero in Vietnam, he'd let me alone. I'd be able to marry you and we'd live on the Crescent, raise kids and cattle."

"Oh, Garrett, you never told me all that...."

"I was afraid it wouldn't work out." Garrett shrugged. "And it didn't. Gus pretended that it wasn't a big deal that I was with you, but it must have been. I'm sure he wanted to hand-pick my wife. He made a point of sending me the Tarrant paper every week and pretty soon, I saw the announcement of your marriage to Hal. Then after I left the army, started my career, he was after me constantly to marry." Garrett looked up. "But you were the only one I wanted, and you were already married."

Her hand lifted to cover her eyes. "I'm so sorry. It must have hurt you."

"Yeah, but if I'd known you were carrying my baby when you married Hal, it would have killed me," he admitted. "So it's probably just as well."

"Why do you think he kept those letters I wrote to you?" Mary Jane asked. "He must have realized you would find them someday and be furious with him."

"I don't know. Maybe at one time he considered using them as blackmail to force you out. If you'd been more specific in the letter, saying that you were pregnant rather than just asking to see me, he probably would have done exactly that."

Mary Jane's shoulders slumped. "He was a sad, bitter man. It's ironic that all I've ever felt for him is pity and sorrow. I never hated him the way he hated me and my family."

"That's a good thing, don't you think?" Garrett said with a slight smile. "Otherwise you and your family might have been plagued by the same kind of bitterness that warped him."

Mary Jane shuddered. It was unthinkable.

Garrett looked up and met her eyes, then stepped closer. The agony was clearing from his face and he smiled at her. "So now what? Where do we go from here?"

"Now?" Heartened by the change in his expression, Mary Jane gave a disbelieving laugh. "Now we become grandparents."

She reached out a hand, and with a rush, Garrett swept her into his arms. He covered her face with kisses. "We can do it if we do it together," he said, touching his lips to her eyes, her cheeks, her mouth. "Hell, we're still young. We can do anything. I've waited a lifetime for you, MarJay. I love you. Please say you'll marry me."

Joy flooded through her. "Yes, Garrett. There was always a part of me that loved you even when I was young and frightened and mad at you for abandoning me so coldly. I'll be glad to marry you now." She laughed as she stood on her tiptoes and wrapped her arms around his shoulders. "After all, we've lost a lot of time, but we're entering a new millennium. What could be better than spending it together?"

Garrett kissed her again, then still holding her, swung her toward the couch and made a grab for his jacket. Digging in the pocket, he produced the ring box. "*Now* will you let me put this on your finger?"

She held up her left hand. "Absolutely. But you've got to marry me fast, Garrett Blackhawk. This grandma's not getting any younger."

He slipped the ring on her finger, then grinned wickedly as he fell onto the couch with her on his lap. "My my, grandma. What big eyes you have."

She batted her eyelashes at him. "The better to flirt with you, my dear."

He lifted her arms and draped them over his shoulders. "And what luscious lips you have."

She gave him a seductive smile and nibbled at his jaw. "The better to kiss you with, my dear."

Garrett's smile grew devilish as he fell back and pulled her to sprawl over him. His hands slid down to cup her bottom. ''And what a great body you've got.''

Mary Jane lifted herself up to kiss him again. ''Grandmas aren't what they used to be, my dear.''

''Something old?'' Shannon asked Mary Jane. Ever practical, she had a checklist for the wedding and was ticking off completed items as she drilled her family on their responsibilities. As she waited for her mother's answer, she gave her winter-white wool dress an approving look.

Dutifully, Mary Jane held up the Bible that had belonged to Garrett's mother. He had found it in this room, the little sitting area on the second floor of his father's ranch house and insisted Mary Jane carry it. She was happy to do so, knowing it brought him happy memories.

It was New Year's Day, and they were to be married in the cleared-out living room of the Blackhawk Ranch. Mary Jane's family and many friends were in attendance, still somewhat shocked, but all present. Garrett and Mary Jane had chosen the location because they felt it would finally put to rest the pain of the past and the betrayal of Gus Blackhawk and Mary Jane's own father, too.

As predicted, the truth of Shannon's parentage had swept through town. Gossips had a field day with it, but Garrett had let it be known that all the money he had contributed to projects around Tarrant would be withdrawn if there was any viciousness attached to the stories. Wisely, the tales had died down and the townspeople were quickly caught up in their own holidays. The doings of the Kellehers didn't seem so important, after all.

Best of all, Shannon had accepted it and was enthusiastic about the marriage.

"Something new?" she asked, the pen poised over the list.

"There's new snow all over the ground outside," Brittnie pointed out. She leaned close to the mirror and fluffed her curly blonde hair.

"Doesn't count," Shannon answered. "Mother? Something new?"

"I have a new dress, new shoes, new hat," she said, pointing to the small, veiled hat that matched her dress. "New hairdo, manicure." She still couldn't believe that one. She gazed in admiration at her shiny nails—smooth, unbroken, polished in pale pink for the first time in many years. Smiling softly, she looked at her daughters. "New me."

It was true. Since she and Garrett had decided to marry, everything in her life had changed. He had hired managers for both ranches, paying them wages that had nearly made her heart stop, but he'd pointed out that they were preserving the heritage of their families for their grandchildren and that was worth any amount of money. She and Garrett would be living in his house in Albuquerque with frequent trips back to Tarrant to see their family.

With an understanding nod, Shannon finally went on. "Something borrowed?"

"I say we borrow some rope from the barn and tie Shannon up 'til she promises to lose that list she's got," Becca grumbled, peeking over Shannon's shoulder to see how many more items needed to be marked off before they could go ahead with the actual wedding. ''Can we hurry this part up? Clay and the kids are waiting for me. I'm sure Christina's giving her dad heart failure by trying to climb the stairs, and Jimmy's going to squirm right out of his new suit. Besides, I know Garrett's waiting for Mom.''

''Be nice,'' Shannon muttered, studying her list. ''I'm an expectant mother.''

Becca and Brittnie exchanged a dry look, then grinned at how their level-headed sister had begun using that excuse to get her way. They never would have expected it of her. They were stunned that Luke seemed to fall for it every time.

''I borrowed a lace handkerchief from your Aunt Kat,'' Mary Jane answered, pulling the gossamer thing from her pocket and dabbing at her eyes which had a tendency to fill with happy tears when she looked at her children.

''Something blue?''

Mary Jane held up the bouquet of blue irises.

With a sigh of satisfaction, Shannon snapped her little notebook shut and nodded. ''We're ready. Where's Uncle Dave?''

''He's where any sensible man would be,'' Brittnie said. ''As far from you and your list as possible.''

''We need to go get him,'' Shannon said, pulling her sisters in for a last minute hug with their mother, then standing back. Misty-eyed, she said, ''Let's get this show on the road.''

The three of them swept out, laughing and teasing, leaving Mary Jane to listen to the echo of their voices as they joined the throng of well-wishers downstairs.

Excited, nervous, and yet peaceful, she waited for her brother to come and offer his arm for the trip down the aisle. He had come from Denver to give her away, though he'd questioned Garrett thoroughly, saying he was only being a conscientious big brother. Mary Jane had been surprised he hadn't challenged Garrett to an arm-wrestling competition.

Within moments, Dave joined her, taking her hand and folding it gently over his arm, securing it there gently and taking her downstairs.

Nervous and excited, Mary Jane stepped toward Garrett who stood before the fireplace with the same minister who had spoken at Gus's funeral. Her gaze swept her family, thrilled at the way they had turned out, pleased that her daughters had become strong women in their own right, and married men who were good enough for them—Becca with Clay, her two children beside her; Brittnie grinning up at Jared; Shannon with Luke's arm forming a protective support behind her. Their lives wouldn't be easy, but they would be full. She said a silent thanks to Hal Kelleher for giving her these wonderful women to be her daughters.

She knew Gus Blackhawk would have hated having her and her family in his house, would have hated that she was marrying Garrett.

Her eyes lifted to Garrett, seeing only his handsome, smiling face, his searing blue eyes fixed on her. She loved him and they would have a wonderful life together. What Gus Blackhawk would have hated didn't matter. It simply didn't matter at all.

# COMING NEXT MONTH

## KIDS IS A 4-LETTER WORD by Stephanie Bond

When Jo Montgomery found herself having to take three kids to the most important meeting in her career, she was frantic. Then she met the children's father, gorgeous widower John Sterling, and she knew her troubles had just begun...

## MARRIAGE FOR MAGGIE by Trisha David

When Devlin Macafferty and his small son literally crash-land onto Maggie's private island, they're both in need of refuge. And as Devlin soon comes to realise, desperately in need of a woman like Maggie too...

## THE BABY PLAN by Liz Fielding

Amanda's biological clock was ticking away furiously— and when she met gorgeous Daniel Redford, she began to fantasise about him as the father of her baby. Determinedly, she set her plan in motion. But she hadn't counted on falling in love...

## THE BRIDAL SWAP by Leigh Michaels

Had Jax Montgomery's fiancée got cold feet—or was Jax having second thoughts? Either way he needed a replacement bride—and was most insistent that, since he'd hired Kara as his wedding organiser, she must be the one to take on the role...

### *Available from 7th January 2000*

*Available at most branches of WH Smith, Tesco, Martins, Borders, Easons, Volume One/James Thin and most good paperback bookshops*

# COMING NEXT MONTH

MILLS & BOON®

*Enchanted*™

## A GOOD WIFE by Betty Neels

Matilda tries to ignore her attraction to Dr. Henry Lovell. After all, he's her boss and engaged to someone else! But soon Henry starts to find Matilda just as intriguing as she finds him…

## THE BRIDESMAID'S BET by Christie Ridgway

Francesca wanted to get married, so she started taking lessons in seduction from brooding bachelor, Brett Swenson, whom she'd always loved from afar. But once this marriage-resistant man claimed her as his own would he ever see her as a potential bride?

## VACANCY: WIFE by Shannon Waverly

Meg's boss had a strict policy to keep romance out of the work place. But, when he took her on a family weekend away, he seemed to see her in a new light. But Meg couldn't allow him to get too close, or he'd discover the secret she'd been keeping from him…

## THE LATIN AFFAIR by Sophie Weston

Nicky hasn't allowed a man to get close to her since she was fifteen and a passionate kiss with an older man ended disastrously. How then can she explain her attraction to Esteban Tremain? Is it that he somehow reminds her of that previous moonlit encounter…?

### Available from 7th January 2000

*Available at most branches of WH Smith, Tesco, Martins, Borders, Easons, Volume One/James Thin and most good paperback bookshops*

# FREE
# 4 BOOKS
## AND A SURPRISE GIFT!

We would like to take this opportunity to thank you for reading this Mills & Boon® book by offering you the chance to take FOUR more specially selected titles from the Enchanted™ series absolutely FREE! We're also making this offer to introduce you to the benefits of the Reader Service™—

★ FREE home delivery        ★ FREE gifts and competitions
★ FREE monthly Newsletter    ★ Exclusive Reader Service discounts
★ Books available before they're in the shops

Accepting these FREE books and gift places you under no obligation to buy; you may cancel at any time, even after receiving your free shipment. Simply complete your details below and return the entire page to the address below. *You don't even need a stamp!*

**YES!** Please send me 4 free Enchanted books and a surprise gift. I understand that unless you hear from me, I will receive 6 superb new titles every month for just £2.40 each, postage and packing free. I am under no obligation to purchase any books and may cancel my subscription at any time. The free books and gift will be mine to keep in any case.

N9EC

Ms/Mrs/Miss/Mr ......................................................Initials ........................
BLOCK CAPITALS PLEASE

Surname ....................................................................................................

Address ....................................................................................................

.................................................................................................................

.............................................................Postcode .......................................

**Send this whole page to:**
**UK: FREEPOST CN81, Croydon, CR9 3WZ**
**EIRE: PO Box 4546, Kilcock, County Kildare (stamp required)**

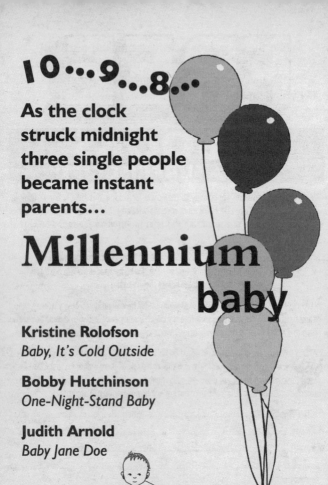